ALSO BY STEWART GILES:

THE DS JASON SMITH SERIES –

- Smith
- Boomerang
- Ladybird
- Occam's Razor
- Harlequin
- Selene
- Horsemen
- Unworthy
- Phobia

THE DC HARRIET TAYLOR SERIES -

- The Beekeeper
- The Perfect Murder
- The Backpacker

For Keith Giles -

14.01.1942 - 18.11.2017.

The likes of whom, very few people

Will have the privilege to encounter.

PREFACE

"She's far too small for that one," the woman told the father of the 6-month-old girl who was about to be positioned on the swing in the playground at the far edge of the park.
"I'll hold on to her," the father promised. "We've done it before, haven't we, sweetheart?" He cast his daughter a knowing glance.
"Just don't drop her now."

The park was starting to fill up. Like-minded parents were making the most of the final days of what had been a very hot summer. Very soon, October would arrive and the chill of early autumn would set in over the city of York.

The father of the baby stood close to the precious cargo on the swing and held her tightly as he rocked her back and forth.
"Is that thing even safe?" the woman asked. "It squeaks. It needs oiling if you ask me."
"It's fine. I've got hold of her."
The father held the swing at head-height and slowly lowered it to the ground. He repeated the process, this time daring to increase the speed of the descent. The baby let out a cry of delight.
"See, she loves it," he called out.

The woman sat down on a bench and took out her phone. On the screen was a recent photograph of her, her husband and their baby girl. The rusty swing continued to rise up and down. Each time it reached the ground a high pitched squeak could be heard.
She's in safe hands, the woman decided and checked for messages on her phone. *We're both in safe hands.*

The woman's eyes left the phone and she glanced across at her baby on the swing. A wave of utter contentment washed over her whole body. This was what she'd always dreamed of – they were the perfect family. She wanted the feeling to last forever. The man lifted the baby from the swing, walked over to the bench and sat down.

He placed the girl on her mother's lap. "See, there's not a scratch on her."

The woman put her phone away and kissed her daughter on the top of her head.

"I won't let anything bad happen to either of you," the man added. "Never."

The mother, the father, and the six-month-old girl were oblivious to the fact that one of them would be dead before the end of the week.

CHAPTER ONE

"Jason," DC Erica Whitton said for the third time in the space of a minute. "Let her go to sleep."

"She doesn't want to go to sleep," DS Jason Smith said.

"It's three in the morning."

"I don't think she knows that. I'm not tired. You go back to sleep."

Laura, Smith and Whitton's baby was lying in her cot at the end of the bed. Her eyes were wide open and she was holding her dad's thumb between her tiny fingers.

"I think she's hungry," Smith suggested.

"She's not hungry," Whitton turned over in the bed. "She had some milk an hour ago. She needs to learn that night time is for sleeping. She really needs some training."

"She's not a dog, Erica. I'll take her for a walk around the house."

Whitton sighed and closed her eyes. She was too tired to argue.

Laura Smith had been born almost six months earlier to the day in York City hospital to two of York's finest detectives. Her sleeping habits aside, she'd so far proved to be a content and happy baby.

"Come on, mate," Smith picked her up and held her close to his chest. "Let's see what Theakston and Fred are up to."

He looked at Whitton and smiled. She was breathing deeply – she was obviously asleep.

Theakston and Fred were snuggled together on the sofa in the living room. The Bull Terrier and the repulsive Pug had formed an instant bond when they'd been introduced to each other a year earlier and the arrival of the baby had cemented that bond further. Theakston, the Bull Terrier opened an eye when he heard Smith and Laura come in the room but the Pug didn't stir.

"What are we going to do with you?" Smith asked his daughter and sat down on the single seater couch. "Your mother thinks you need some training."
Both dogs were now snoring loudly on the sofa.
"I couldn't train them," Smith pointed to the snoring competition across the room. "What chance have I got with you?"
The clock on the wall read 3:30 yet neither Smith nor his daughter were tired. Smith wasn't due back at work for another week. He'd taken two weeks off to help out – lack of sleep was second nature to him but Whitton was starting to take strain.
"You've taken over our lives," he stroked Laura's hair. "Even the dogs have had to take a back seat."

Smith walked through to the kitchen and made coffee. He placed his daughter in her chair at the table and went outside for a cigarette. There were no clouds in the sky and it was very warm. Autumn still seemed a long way off. He finished the cigarette, flicked the butt over the wall into his neighbour's garden and lit another one. He looked up at the sky. The half-moon cast an eerie glow over the trees at the end of the garden. He thought about how his life had turned out and smiled. If anybody had told him a year ago he would be sitting in the garden while his six-month-old daughter was in the kitchen he would have told them they needed more sleep, yet here he was. And if that same person had told him he would turn into the happiest father in the world, he would have had them committed on the spot. The day that Laura came into the world had been the best day of his life. Whitton had agreed they would name her after Smith's sister. Laura had disappeared from a beach in Western Australia when Smith was a teenager. They met up briefly ten years later and then her body was found in the River Ouse. Smith always thought he'd never be able to enjoy family life again – all his relations were dead but Laura junior had changed everything.

Smith stubbed out the cigarette and went back inside. Laura was still wide awake. She was showing no sign of weariness. Smith picked her out of the seat and she started to make quiet gurgling sounds.

"We need to sleep, mate," he carried her up the stairs.

Whitton was snoring quietly in bed. Smith carefully moved the duvet to one side and crept in next to her. Laura was still clutched to his chest.

CHAPTER TWO

Smith was in a deep sleep when his mobile phone started to ring. Laura was still lying on his chest – she hadn't moved at all in the night. Whitton stirred in the bed next to them. She smiled and shook her head when she saw Smith with the baby fast asleep on his chest.

"Wake up," she shook Smith and picked up Laura. "Your phone's been ringing for ages."

Smith opened his eyes, sat up in bed and picked up the phone.

"It's work. I don't think I want to answer it."

The ringing stopped.

"Just see what they want," Whitton said. "I'm going to sort this little lady out. From that smell I'd say she needs changing."

They left the bedroom as Smith's phone started to ring again.

"Smith," he answered it. "In case you've forgotten, I'm on leave."

"Sarge," it was DC Bridge. "Sorry to bother you but the DI told me to get hold of you."

"What part of I'm on leave does Brownhill not understand?"

"There's been a murder. A young woman's had her brains bashed in."

"I'm not at work for another week, Bridge. Whitton needs some help with the baby – she's quite a handful."

"The DI insists, Sarge. You know what Brownhill's like."

"You and Yang Chu can handle it. You've dealt with plenty of murders before."

"This one's different, Sarge."

"A murder's a murder. I'll see you in a week."

"This one's different," Bridge said again before Smith could ring off. "I think you'd better come and have a look."

* * *

Half an hour later, Smith parked his car outside the address Bridge had given him. Whitton had insisted he go – she knew that Bridge would not have phoned if it wasn't important. Smith got out of the car. Grant Webber's new Volvo was already parked outside the house. The head of forensics was always quick to get to the scene. There was no sign of DI Brownhill's old Citroen.

Smith looked at the front of the house. It was one of the newer houses that had been built at the turn of the century. It was two roads from the river and the houses in this street were generally owned by middle class professionals – doctors and lawyers. Bridge emerged from the house with DC Yang Chu in tow. Yang Chu didn't look too healthy – his face was deathly pale and his eyes were bloodshot.

"That bad is it?" Smith said to Bridge.

"Worse one I've ever seen," Bridge replied. "Yang Chu puked on the carpet in the hallway. Webber wasn't impressed."

"I couldn't make it out there in time," Yang Chu told Smith. "I hope your stomach is strong this morning."

"Let's see, shall we?" Smith walked past them inside the house.

Grant Webber was examining something on the carpet in the hallway. He looked up when he heard Smith approaching.

"Is that Yang Chu's breakfast?" Smith pointed to a stain on the carpet.

"You can't stay away, can you? I thought you were on leave."

"Brownhill's orders. You of all people should know how insistent she can be."

"The dead woman is in the living room. Second door to the left. How's the family bliss going?"

"The baby needs a bit of training, according to Whitton."

"If the poor kid's anything like her dad, she's got no chance. Don't touch anything in there. I'm still waiting for the rest of my team. I just had a quick look when I got here."

Smith donned a pair of gloves and pushed the door open. The unmistakable stench of death hit him immediately. He stood in the doorway and scanned the room. He knew that first impressions were vital in any murder investigation. The curtains were closed and the lights were on. The room was littered with toys – fluffy animals lay on the furniture and rubber rattles and plastic baby toys were scattered all over the carpet. A baby's walking ring sat underneath the window. A milk bottle stood on the coffee table. It was still full of milk. Next to it was a small bowl half-full of what looked like dried brown paint.

The woman was lying on her back in the corner of the room underneath a bookshelf. An electric iron lay on the floor next to her. Smith breathed in deeply and moved in to get a closer look. He could see straight away why Yang Chu's stomach had reacted like it did. The woman had no face left. The cartilage from her crushed nose was now mixed with the dried blood on her exposed cheekbones. Her eyes had been forced into the back of her head and where her mouth once was, was now just a gaping hole. Bridge had been right – this was the worst one Smith had ever seen.

"It looks like they left the murder weapon for us," Webber appeared in the doorway and Smith flinched. "At least that's something."
"Where's the baby?" Smith turned around to face him.
"With a neighbour. I see you haven't lost your touch while you've been away. What do you make of the woman's face?"
"Whoever did this was pissed off. They acted with quite a fury. Her face has been caved in. Surely a good whack to the back of the head would have been enough."
"Probably," Webber agreed.
"I reckon she was killed last night. The curtains were closed and the lights were left on. Do we know who she is?"

"That's not my job – you know that." Webber looked at his watch. "Where the hell is my team?" He took out his mobile phone and left the room.

Smith looked again at what was once a woman's face and paced around the room. He stopped by the milk bottle and frowned. It was about time for Laura's feed. Whitton would be preparing the formula while he stood there in a room with a badly mutilated woman. The woman's baby would now have to grow up without a mother. He bent down to the bowl containing the paint and sniffed. The contents in the bowl had an acrid, metallic odour. Smith knew that smell very well.

"Webber," he shouted. "Get in here now.

Webber appeared. "What?"

"This is definitely not paint," Smith pointed to the contents of the bowl. "It's blood. You can check it but I'm pretty sure it's blood."

Webber sniffed the bowl.

"You're right."

"What's a bowl of blood doing in here?" Smith thought out loud and approached the window. He opened the curtains with one swift tug.

"What the hell…" Webber gasped at the writing on the window.

The word *UNWORTHY* had been written in dark-red block capitals on the glass.

CHAPTER THREE

Smith stood outside the house and lit a cigarette. He inhaled deeply and felt the buzz of the first smoke of the day rush through his veins. Bridge and Yang Chu walked up to him. Yang Chu's face had regained some of its colour.

"What do we know?" Smith exhaled a cloud of smoke.

"The woman's name is Julie Phelps," Bridge told him. "Twenty-six years old."

"Who found her?"

"The next-door neighbour. He'd come round to complain about the noise."

"Noise?"

"Mrs Phelps has a six-month old baby boy. The neighbour said the baby started screaming at around nine last night and didn't stop."

"I see. What about the husband? The father of the baby? Where's he now?"

"He's on his way. He was at a school reunion in Newcastle last night and he stayed over with some friends."

"Did you see her face?" Yang Chu asked. "That's the worst thing I've ever seen."

"There was a word written on the window," Smith told them. "The word, *UNWORTHY*."

"Unworthy?" Bridge repeated.

"It looks like it was written in the woman's blood."

"Unworthy," Bridge said once more. "Why would somebody write that on the window?"

"I have no idea," Smith said. "We'll have more info when the husband gets here."

"What do you think happened, Sarge?" Yang Chu asked.

"The curtains were closed so I think she was killed last night some time. Probably around the same time the baby started to scream. There was an untouched bottle of milk on the table. The poor child was probably hungry. I know – Laura's like a bear with a sore head when she hasn't had enough to eat."

"How's the family life going, Sarge?" Bridge said. "I bet Whitton's driving you up the wall."

"Unworthy?" Smith ignored his question. "Why would somebody bash a woman's face in and write 'Unworthy' on the windowpane in blood?"

DI Brownhill parked behind Smith's Ford Sierra and got out the car. Smith noticed straight away that there was something different about her – she'd lost a bit of weight and as she got closer he could see that the growth of hair that usually decorated her top lip was gone.

"Morning, boss," Smith said. "You look nice. You look almost feminine."

Yang Chu started to giggle.

"Sorry to drag you into this," Brownhill said. "Have you had a look inside yet?"

"I have."

"Then you'll understand why you were called in. What do we know?"

Smith told her about the word written on the window.

"Unworthy?" Brownhill said when Smith was finished. "What do you think it means?"

"Unfit, ma'am," Yang Chu offered. "Undeserving."

"I'm not asking for a Thesaurus definition, detective. Why would somebody write it on the woman's window?"

"In blood, too," Bridge added.

"The husband is due back soon," Smith told her. "I'm sure he'll be able to tell us more about her."

"OK," Brownhill said. "Is Grant still inside the house?"

"He's waiting for the rest of his team. They need to check the window. I'm sure it was written with a finger dipped in blood."

"Grant knows his job. Where's the baby now?"

"With the neighbour. The poor thing probably saw the whole thing."

"I doubt we'll get much out of a six-month old kid," Yang Chu said.

"Of course we won't," Brownhill scoffed. "This is what we're going to do. It's probably going to be a good few hours before Grant and his team can give us anything and we also have to wait for the husband to arrive. Smith, seeing as though you're officially back in the thick of things, you and Bridge can speak with the neighbour who found her. See if he heard anything else other than a crying baby last night. Yang Chu, you and me are going to see if the neighbours on the other side of the street heard anything unusual last night."

CHAPTER FOUR

Elizabeth Watson answered the door straight away. She was still wearing her dressing gown. The sound of a baby crying could be heard from inside the house.

"Mrs Watson," Smith said. "DS Smith and this is DC Bridge. That little chap in there doesn't sound too happy. Can we have a word?"

"I can't seem to calm him down. It's as though he knows what's happened to his mother. You'd better come in."

Smith and Bridge followed her inside. A thin man with a moustache was holding the baby boy in the air in the hallway.

"It's alright, Harry," he said in a soft voice. "Everything's going to be alright." He looked at Smith. "He hasn't stopped crying all night. I don't know what to do. Babies aren't really my strong point, I'm afraid."

"Brian," Elizabeth said. "These men are from the police. They need to talk to you."

The baby still wouldn't stop crying.

"Give him here." Smith held out his hands.

Elizabeth seemed concerned. The look in her eyes showed that she didn't think Smith looked like a man to trust with a baby.

"Don't worry," Smith noted the expression on her face. "I've got one of these at home – a six-month old girl called Laura."

He held out his hands and Mr Watson handed him the baby.

"Hey, little fella," Smith said. "You're a lot heavier than my little girl. And she eats like a horse. Harry, isn't it?"

Elizabeth nodded.

"Well, Harry." Smith stroked the baby's hair. "How about Mrs Watson gets you something to eat and we go and have a word with Mr Watson? Let's see if we can find out what happened to your Mom."

Harry seemed fascinated with Smith's face. He reached out a hand and touched the DS's nose.

"Hey," Smith grimaced. "You've got quite a grip on you there." He handed the baby to Mrs Watson. He'd stopped crying and a smile had appeared on his face.

"Babies seem to like me," Smith said. "For some strange reason. Dogs too. I must have one of those faces."

"We can go through to the living room," Brian suggested.

"You were the one who found Mrs Phelps last night?" Smith said when Brian Watson had closed the door to the living room. "Is that right?"

"The baby was screaming his head off. I went round to see if everything was OK. It sounded like Julie had left him on his own."

"What time was this?" Bridge asked.

"Around ten, I think. That little tyke has a good set of lungs on him, I can tell you that. I went next door. The door was open."

"Open as in unlocked?" Smith asked.

"Open as in wide open. I knocked anyway but there was no answer. I called out for Julie and went inside. I found her in the living room. Who on earth would want to do such a thing? With the baby in the same room?"

"We'll find out," Smith promised. "You said you thought Julie had left the baby on his own – was she in the habit of leaving Harry to fend for himself?"

"No... I mean sometimes."

"Go on."

"I've noticed that she sometimes goes out to the shops without the baby. She doesn't leave him for long – an hour at the most."

"Maybe her husband looks after Harry when she goes out," Bridge suggested.

"John works during the week. No, she leaves Harry on his own."

"OK," Smith said. "I don't think that's relevant right now. You found her around ten last night. Did you hear anything else other than the baby crying? Anything strange?"

"Anything strange?"

"Raised voices. Sounds that may suggest a struggle was taking place?"

"No. I turned up the TV to drown out the crying. Not that it helped. That kid has a hell of a scream on him."

"Do you know the Phelps' well?" Bridge asked.

"John's lived next door to us for over ten years. He's always been a courteous and quiet neighbour. He married Julie just over a year ago, and she moved in straight away. Harry was already on the way when they got married. I've done the maths."

"Can you think of anybody who would want to hurt Mrs Phelps?" Smith said.

"No. Julie was a bit wild in her day, but I can't think that anybody would want to do this to her. Did you see her face?"

"What do you mean by *wild*?" Smith asked.

"You know – drinking, partying until the early hours in the morning. She had a bit of a reputation if you know what I mean. She seemed to calm down when she met John, though. I'm sure she was a good mother in her own way."

"Thank you for your time, Mr Watson." Smith stood up and Bridge did the same. "That poor child is going to need his father."

"What do you think, Sarge?" Bridge said outside the house. "Julie Phelps sounds like quite a lively one."

"Let's see what her husband has to say. How's the swotting going?"

Bridge had been studying for the sergeant's examination. Since Detective Sergeant Alan Thompson had succumbed to cancer the year before, the DS position had come up for grabs. Bridge and Yang Chu had both decided to apply.

"I can't get my head around some of it," Bridge admitted. "Some of that stuff is quite baffling."

"And you'll probably forget most of it within a year and you'll never put it into practice. Do yourself a favour though – ease off on the womanising for at least until the exam's over. That stuff is quite intensive and you're going to need your wits about you."

"I still think it's unfair that Yang Chu was allowed to apply. He's only been here five minutes."

"He's a bloody good detective. Besides, it's good to have a bit of competition – it gives you a bit of a kick up the arse."

A white Nissan SUV drove up and parked outside the Phelps's house. A tall man got out and walked up to Smith and Bridge. His face was very pale and his eyes were bloodshot.

"Mr Phelps?" Smith said.

"I came as soon as I could," he said and Smith caught a whiff of stale alcohol on his breath. "Where's Julie?"

"Still inside the house," Smith said. "There's an ambulance on the way."

"What about Harry?"

"He's with the Watsons," Bridge told him. "He's being well looked after."

"We're very sorry for your loss, Mr Phelps," Smith said.

"Please, call me John. Can I see my wife?"

Smith didn't think that was such a good idea – Julie Phelps's face had been caved in. There wasn't much left of it. "I don't think you should go in just yet."

"What the hell happened?"

"We still don't know. Brian Watson heard the baby crying last night and went to check to see if everything was alright. That's when he found her."

"I can't believe this is happening," John looked like he was about to pass out. His face was even paler now. He took a deep breath and sat down on the small wall in front of the house.

"Is there someone we can call?" Bridge said. "A friend or family member?"

"No. I just want to see my wife."

An ambulance pulled up outside, and two paramedics got out the back. Smith walked up to them.

"DS Smith," he took out his ID. "She's in there." He pointed to the Phelps's house. "I have to warn you, her face is a bit of a mess. Her husband is sitting on the wall there. Do me a favour and cover her up – he shouldn't have to see her like that."

"We have been briefed," one of the paramedics said rather gruffly.

He helped his colleague take a stretcher from the back and went inside the house. A few minutes later, they reappeared with Julie Phelps. She'd been covered with a black blanket.

"Where are they taking her?" her husband asked Bridge.

"To the hospital," Bridge said. "I'm afraid we need to find out exactly what happened to her."

"Can I at least go inside my house, now?"

"Forensics are still busy in there. They shouldn't be long."

Grant Webber and his team came out the house right on cue. Webber nodded to Smith to indicate he wanted to talk.

"All done," he said. "I had one of my guys clean the window. The husband shouldn't have to see that. We've got everything we need. Are you back at work for good now?"

"Looks like it," Smith replied. "Let us know what you find out."

"This is a nasty one. I really don't like the look of this one. Did you see that woman's face?"

"I did. How's it going with you and the DI? I couldn't believe it when I saw her this morning. She really seems to be making an effort to look like a woman. She must really like you."
"I'll let you know what we find out as soon as possible." The head of forensics walked off shaking his head.

CHAPTER FIVE

Brownhill and Yang Chu had drawn a blank with the neighbours on the other side of the Phelps' house to the Watsons. None of them had seen or heard anything other than the sound of the baby crying. The lady next door had informed them that Harry's screaming was a regular occurrence, especially late at night. Everybody the DI and Yang Chu had spoken to appeared to have the same opinion of Julie Phelps, however. Her husband, John was ten years older than her and theirs was a whirlwind romance. The wedding had been a spur of the moment thing when they'd found out about the baby. One of the neighbours even suggested the baby probably wasn't even John's.

* * *

"It sounds like she was a bit of a tart," Yang Chu said back at the station. Smith, Bridge and PC Baldwin were drinking coffee in the canteen.
"Yang Chu," Baldwin said. "That's a horrible thing to say."
"It's the truth. Everybody who knew her thought the same thing. She'd drop her knickers for the price of half a pint apparently."
"Mr and Mrs Watson reckoned she changed when she met her husband," Bridge said. "She became more responsible."
"A leopard doesn't change its spots," Yang Chu insisted. "And a tart's a tart."
"That's enough," Baldwin said. "The woman's barely cold."

Smith hadn't said a word since they sat down in the canteen. He was staring out of the window. There wasn't a cloud in the sky. It was a perfect day for an outing to the park. Whitton, Laura, Theakston, Fred and himself. The sun beating down on their backs. But now he was stuck in the canteen at the station listening to an argument about whether a woman who'd had her face caved in was a tart or not.
"Unworthy," he said suddenly.

"Sarge?" Bridge said.

"The word written on Julie Phelps's window in her blood. Unworthy. Somebody killed her because they believed her to be unworthy. Unworthy of what?"

"Being a mother?" Yang Chu suggested.

"Or a wife?" Bridge added.

"Or both," Smith said. "She was killed in such a violent way that it suggests that whoever did this really hated her for whatever they believed her to be unworthy of if that makes any sense. And the fact that they wrote on the window means they wanted her unworthiness to be noted. They wanted us to see it."

"And why write it in blood?" Bridge said.

"To make it all the more symbolic," Baldwin chipped in.

The three detectives stared at her.

"What?" she said.

"Since when did you start coming up with stuff like that?" Bridge asked.

"Stuff like what? I reckon the fact that it was written in blood suggests the killer wanted to hammer home his message. It wasn't enough to just kill her and write the word – it had to have some emphasis. Hence the blood."

"Well bugger me," Yang Chu said. "I've heard everything now. The girl from the front desk is a closet shrink."

"Yang Chu," Smith said. "That's enough. Baldwin has a valid point there and I agree with her. We'll know for a fact if it was indeed Julie Phelps's blood when Webber has finished but I'm ninety nine percent sure it is."

DI Brownhill came in.

"I thought I'd find you all in here," she said. "Smith, welcome back. I know you were supposed to be off for another week but it can't be helped. We need all the experienced officers we can muster on this one. Baldwin, could you get back to work, please. I'd hate for the Super to walk in and find the front desk unattended."

"Yes, ma'am," Baldwin sighed and left the room.

"Boss," Smith said to Brownhill. "I have something I want to put past you."

"I don't like the sound of this."

"It's about Baldwin."

"Go on."

"She's wasted behind a desk. I want her on this investigation."

"You've got to be kidding. What does she know about murder investigations?"

"A lot more than we give her credit for." He told her what they'd been discussing before she came in.

"And you think she can handle it?" Brownhill said when Smith was finished.

"I know she can. You said yourself that we need everyone we've got on this. Whitton isn't coming back for months. Baldwin has been involved in just about every murder investigation we've had to deal with. In one way or another. She's proven herself. She's ready."

"I'll give it some thought."

"We haven't got time for thoughts. Get her started. What time is John Phelps coming in?"

"In about three hours. He wanted to leave it until tomorrow but I made it clear that time is of the essence. We need to speak to him as soon as possible."

"Good. Then you've got three hours to make up your mind about Baldwin. I want her to sit in with me when I interview Mr Phelps."

"Have you forgotten who the superior officer is here, Smith?"

"How could I ever forget? I'll see you in two hours."

"Where are you going?"

"Home. And as I've cut my leave short to be here, I think you can give me a couple of hours to go home and explain everything to Whitton. I want to keep her in the loop."

Smith stood up and left the canteen before the DI had a chance to argue.

* * *

Whitton was in the garden with Laura and the two dogs when Smith got home. Theakston, the Bull Terrier and Fred, the grotesque Pug were lying on a blanket next to Laura. Theakston started to growl when Smith came closer. The Pug couldn't seem to care less.

"It's me, you dope," Smith said to Theakston.

"He's so protective over her." Whitton picked Laura up and handed her to Smith. "I hate to know what he'd do if someone tried to attack her. How was it?"

"Worst one I've ever seen." Smith kissed his daughter on the top of her head. "She'd had her face caved in with an electric iron. There wasn't much left of it. The word *UNWORTHY* was written on the window in her blood, too."

"Unworthy?"

"She was a bit of a goer by all accounts. Baldwin thinks the word written in blood was symbolic."

"Baldwin? What's she got to do with anything?"

"I think it's about time she did something else apart from manning the front desk. She's got what it takes to be part of the team, full time. I've given the DI a few hours to agree with me."

Whitton sighed. "I wish I was there to help."

"You can help here. With Thompson yet to be replaced and you on maternity leave, we're extremely short-staffed. I had to go back."

"I wouldn't expect you to do anything else. I just feel a bit useless at the moment."

Smith placed Laura back on the blanket. "This little lady doesn't think you're useless and neither do I. I'll keep you in the loop. You may be a mother now but you're also a brilliant detective."

"How's the DS rivalry panning out? I bet Bridge is a bit pissed off that they didn't just give it to him?"

"A bit. Yang Chu deserves it, though. He's proven himself. Can we talk about something else for an hour or so? The murdered woman's husband is due at the station at 3. I'd quite like to take my mind off things until then."

Smith lit a cigarette and walked to the end of the garden. His neighbour was pruning his roses next door.

"Afternoon," Smith exhaled a cloud of smoke. "Beautiful day."

"That's going to aggravate my asthma," the man pointed to Smith's cigarette. "Would you mind blowing your smoke somewhere else? You shouldn't be smoking in front of the baby, anyway."

"You've missed one," Smith pointed to a dead rose, stubbed out his cigarette and went back to join his family.

CHAPTER SIX

Gordon Turner was running late. He had a 3pm meeting at the bank. Gordon had a lot riding on the meeting – it could determine whether his business would close or whether it would be able to survive for another year at least. He ran a small grocery store on the outskirts of the city. Even though he'd diversified and started offering a wider range of products, the combination of the global downturn in the economy and the weight behind the huge chain stores was dragging him under.

The bank manager hadn't sounded too positive either – banks were reluctant to lend to smaller businesses these days and the new credit regulations didn't exactly help matters.

"I can handle the delivery," May told him. "Get going. It won't do your chances of getting the loan any favours if you're late. I can handle the delivery."

May was a part-timer at the grocery store. She'd been with Gordon for five years.

"Just check the stock," Gordon told her. "They've tried to rip us off in the past. Don't sign the delivery note until you've checked the stock."

"I have done this before. Get off to the bank. And good luck."

Good luck, Gordon thought as he got in his car and turned the key in the ignition. *I need more than a bit of luck – I need a bloody miracle.*

He was right. Gordon was fifty eight years old and he still rented a flat. The only collateral he was able to come up with was the future earnings from the store and he knew very well that no self respecting bank manager would risk lending on that basis.

He turned left onto the High Street and carried on for a mile or so. The clock on the dashboard read 2:45. Gordon still had to find parking by the bank and he knew how long that could take sometimes. He increased his speed and opened the window. He was starting to sweat. He turned onto the road that ran through the new housing estate. The houses had been built a few years earlier. From the cars parked on the road outside the modern face-brick properties, Gordon could tell there was money here – a lot of money. Gordon knew very little about cars but he knew the shiny SUVs and sports cars on display would cost him more than he could expect to earn in a very long time – more than the loan he was rushing to the bank to procure, even. The idea made him angry.

Where has all this money come from?

He was about to take the road that led towards the city centre when he spotted something out of the corner of his eye. The child appeared from behind a parked car and Gordon slammed on the brakes. The car screeched to a halt and Gordon turned off the engine. He wiped the sweat from his forehead and got out. In front of him stood a small boy. He couldn't have been more than three or four years old. He was barefoot and dressed in a blue all-in-one jumper suit. There was blood all over his face. He had more blood on his hands and feet. Gordon's heart started to beat faster.

I've hit a child with my car.

He thought he'd managed to stop in time and he hadn't heard a thud when he hit the boy.

"Mammy," the boy said.

"Are you OK?" Gordon asked.

He couldn't see any obvious injuries on the child. The boy standing there was apparently unhurt.

"Mammy," the boy said again and held out a blood-stained hand.

"Jonathan," a voice came from behind Gordon. "What happened?"

Gordon turned round and stood face to face with a middle-aged woman.

"Jonathan," she said again. "Are you alright? Why's he covered in blood?" she said to Gordon. "Did you hit him with your car?"

"No," Gordon couldn't believe what was happening. "He appeared from behind that car there. I stopped in time. I didn't hit him. I don't think it's blood. It must be paint."

"Mammy," Jonathan said once more.

"Let's get you home," the woman took hold of his hand and led him away. From the way he walked it was clear to Gordon that he was unharmed.

Red paint, Gordon thought as he got back in his car, *bloody red paint.* He was definitely going to be late for his appointment at the bank.

CHAPTER SEVEN

PC Baldwin wasn't manning the desk at the station when Smith walked in. A PC Smith had barely spoken to was talking on the telephone. He appeared to be rather frustrated.

"I assure you, sir, a missing cat is more of a job for the RSPCA." He held the handset away from his ear.

Smith waited for him to end the call.

"Where's Baldwin?" he asked. His name badge read PC Hunter.

"With the DI in Brownhill's office," Hunter said. "Apparently CID are short staffed and she's been called in to help."

Smith smiled. "Thanks, Hunter."

"I didn't join up to sit behind a desk answering phone calls."

"Neither did I." Smith said and walked past him towards the offices.

He knocked on Brownhill's office door and went in. Baldwin was sitting opposite the DI.

"Your wish has been granted," Brownhill said.

"I knew you'd come round to my way of thinking one day."

"It's only a temporary measure, though," Brownhill added. "John Phelps will be here shortly. I've instructed PC Baldwin that she is to merely sit in and observe. She lacks the experience in an interview situation. The poor man has just lost his wife. You saw the woman's face – Mr Phelps will be understandably distraught. I want you to tread carefully. Both of you."

"Boss, with respect, John Phelps is still a suspect in my eyes. I can tread carefully but I also want to rule him out as soon as possible."

"Just try to show a bit of compassion."

"I'm full of compassion. Come on, Baldwin, let's get a cup of coffee before Phelps gets here."

John Phelps arrived half an hour later. He sat in interview room 3 opposite Smith and Baldwin. He looked exhausted.

"Interview with John Phelps commenced 3:15," Smith began. "Present DS Smith and PC Baldwin. Mr Phelps, we're very sorry for your loss. I realise this is extremely difficult but it needs to be done. We intend to find out what happened to your wife and there are some questions that need to be asked."

"I have the names and contact numbers here," Phelps placed a piece of paper on the table in front of Smith. "That's where the reunion took place." He pointed to the paper. "And that's the friend I stayed with in Newcastle last night."

Smith was shocked. "Thank you. We'll check them out. What time did you leave Newcastle?"

"When you lot called about Julie. Dave Lewis will corroborate it. He was with me when I took the call. He's the guy I stayed over with."

"OK," Smith said. "Can you think of anybody who might have wanted to hurt your wife?"

"No. Julie didn't have any enemies that I know of. She was a good mother. I know what some people have been saying about her but that's all in the past. We're all allowed a past aren't we? We all do things we regret later in life don't we?"

"You're dead right there. Could you elaborate for us? What was Julie like before you met her? It could be relevant to what happened to her."

"Julie and I met at work. She was temping for the registrar office. I'm the manager there."

"Registrar office?"

"Births deaths and marriages. Julie was a hard worker. We hit it off straight away despite the difference in our age."

"You're ten years older than her."

"It didn't seem to matter to her. We started going out and we were married within a year. Harry was the best thing to happen to both of us."
His bottom lip started to quiver and Smith was afraid he was going to burst into tears.
"Take your time, Mr Phelps," Baldwin said. "We know this is difficult but could you tell us a bit about Julie's past?"
"She liked to let her hair down a bit. And she had a healthy sexual appetite. I didn't judge her. Why is it that if a woman sleeps around a lot she's some kind of whore but if a man does the same, he's a Casanova?"
"Did Julie talk much about her past?" Smith asked.
"We were both very open with each other. You might not believe it to look at me but I have a few skeletons in the old closet too."
"Do you know if Julie upset anybody recently?" Baldwin said.
"Not really. She's had a hard time fitting in on the street where we live – some of the old prudes don't exactly hide their opinions and Julie wasn't one to hold her tongue but it's mostly old biddies with old-fashioned values. I can't imagine that any of these old ladies would kill her for it."
"And Julie hasn't been acting strange recently?" Smith said.
"Not at all. Harry has taken over our lives – in a very good way. That baby has been a Godsend to both of us. I don't know what I'm going to do now. Julie was a good mother. I don't know what me and Harry are going to do without her."
Smith thought about what he would do if the same thing happened to Whitton and shivered.

"Mr Phelps," he continued. "We're going to need a list of Julie's friends, past and present."
"She kicked most of her old friends into touch. Like I said before, she changed. She didn't hang around with the types she used to – she moved on."

"We'll need that list nevertheless."

"Are you suggesting that one of the old low-life crowd could have done this to her?"

"We don't know," Smith said. "Do you think you can give us some names? You said you were both open with each other. She must have talked about some of the people she used to associate with."

"I'll see what I can do. Will there be anything else? I really need to be with my son right now. We need each other more than ever at the moment."

"That's all for now." Smith looked at his watch. "Interview with John Phelps ended 3:52."

CHAPTER EIGHT

"He didn't do it," Baldwin said to Smith in the corridor when John Phelps had gone home.

"No," Smith agreed. "We'll check out to see if he was in Newcastle anyway but I reckon we need to start looking elsewhere. We'll get onto it as soon as we get that list of his wife's friends."

"How's Whitton doing? I miss having her around here."

"She's feeling left out. I'm going to try and keep her up to date with the investigation. Maybe she won't feel so isolated then."

"Is that such a good idea? This murder is a bit close to home with the baby and everything."

"Whitton has always been able to separate work and home," Smith said and wished he was able to do the same.

It never ceased to amaze him how Whitton could go home after a draining investigation and forget all about it. It was a particular trait of hers he envied.

PC Hunter ran towards them. His eyes were wide and he was very red in the face.

"Sir," he said to Smith. "There's been another murder. A woman has been stabbed in her home. A neighbour just phoned. It's the new estate just off from the river.

"Come on, Baldwin," Smith said. "You're about to be thrown in at the deep end."

* * *

Smith parked his car outside the address PC Hunter had given him. A group of people were gathered in the street outside the house. An elderly lady approached Smith's car and he wound down the window.

"Are you from the police?" she asked even though Baldwin was wearing her uniform.

"DS Smith," Smith told her. "And this is PC Baldwin. What happened?"

"She's in the kitchen." The old lady pointed to a house with a red door. "It's awful. There's blood everywhere. She has a three and a half year old boy."

Smith got out the car and headed for the house. Baldwin followed close behind. The door was ajar. Smith took out a pair of gloves and put them on.

"Do you have any gloves?" he asked Baldwin.

"No," Baldwin replied. "I don't carry gloves with me."

"Stay behind me. And don't touch anything. Webber will have my balls if you contaminate his evidence."

He opened the door further and went inside. There were red footprints on the carpet in the hallway. The feet that made them were very small. Smith followed the footprints and stopped outside the entrance to the kitchen.

"Stay here," he told Baldwin. "And get Webber here now."

He stepped inside the biggest kitchen he had ever seen. A huge granite work-top dominated the centre of the room. There were more tiny footprints on the tiles on the floor. Smith followed them round the work-top and stopped next to a double-door refrigerator. The woman was lying face down next to the stove. Her white nightdress was stained red. There was a pool of blood on the tiles around her. A large carving knife lay on the floor next to her legs.

Smith took a step back, breathed in deeply and looked around the room. The blood appeared to be concentrated on the tiles around the dead woman – there were no spatters on the walls or windows. He made his way back round the work-top and looked at the scene from a different angle. He spotted something on the far side of the granite centrepiece. There was something on a smaller refrigerator in the far corner. He moved closer and saw that the word *Unworthy* had been scratched on the front. The Letters were jagged and contained spots of red.

Grant Webber announced his presence with a cough and Smith turned round.

"What is it with you, Smith?" he said. "Why do murders seem to happen when you're around?"

"It's the same killer," Smith ignored his question. "Look at the fridge."

Webber walked round to where Smith was pointing and knelt down.

"Unworthy? What the hell is going on here?"

"I was hoping you could tell me. There's a carving knife next to the body. From the amount of blood, I'd say she was stabbed more than once. What do you make of the footprints? Do you think our killer had tiny feet?"

"You're losing your touch, Smith. Firstly, the direction of the prints tells us the owner of the feet that made them was walking away from the body."

"And…"

"If you'd bothered to find out, the woman had a young child. Baldwin spoke to the old lady who phoned it in. The child was found walking around outside covered in blood. The old lady thought he'd been hit by a car."

"Why was he covered in blood?"

"You'll have to ask him that, although I doubt you'll get much out of a three and a half year old kid. My guess is, he went to his mother and got covered in blood in the process. What *is* Baldwin doing here anyway?"

"We're short-staffed. I'll leave you to it. I need a smoke."

Smith lit a cigarette outside the house and inhaled deeply.

What the hell is going on? Two women are killed in the space of 24 hours. Both of them had young children. The word Unworthy was written at both murder scenes. There's obviously a connection between the two.

A man in his early thirties walked up. "What's going on?" he asked. "What's happened to young Jonathan? I saw him wandering around covered in blood."

"Who are you?" Smith asked him.

"The name's Lester Green. I live in the house opposite Magda and Jonathan."

"Magda?"

"Magda Collins. Jonathan's mother. What's happened?"

"We don't know yet. You said you live across the road from Magda and Jonathan. What about Jonathan's father? Where's he?"

"He died about a year ago. Cancer. Poor Magda's had to cope on her own although her husband didn't leave her short."

"You said you saw Jonathan wandering around earlier? Covered in blood. What time was this?"

"About an hour ago. I was watering the plants on the windowsill in the lounge in my house across the road. He came out of the house and just walked around aimlessly."

"And you didn't think to help him?"

"There was a screech of a car's brakes and then Mrs King from number ten appeared. She took hold of the boy so I didn't think I needed to interfere – Mrs King seemed to have it under control."

Baldwin came out of the house. "Webber's just about finished." She nodded to Smith. "Can I have a word, Sarge?"

"Thank you for your time, Lester," he said to Mr Green. "We may need to talk to you again."

"I work from home," Green said. "I'm almost always here."

"What's up?" Smith asked Baldwin when Lester Green had gone back inside his house.

"There were no prints on the knife," Baldwin told him. "But Webber got a boot print. It was much bigger than the footprints left by the child – size 12 or 13, Webber thinks."

"A man, then." Smith thought out loud.

"Looks like it."

"Anything else?"

"The writing on the fridge. The letters were scratched deep into the metal. Webber reckons it would have taken quite a bit of strength to do that with a knife."

"Good," Smith said. "You're doing OK, Baldwin. Where's the kid now?"

"Magda Collins' brother is on his way from Harrogate. In the meantime, Jonathan is with a neighbour – a Mrs Frances King. She lives at number ten."

"We need to speak to that young lad."

"He's three and a half years old."

"Then he knows how to talk. I have a way with kids. Let's talk to him before Mrs Collins' brother arrives and throws a spanner in the works."

CHAPTER NINE

Whitton and Laura sat on the bench in the park down the road from Smith's house. The late afternoon sun was beating down on the path next to the lake. Two ducks were engaged in a bobbing competition in the water. The ducklings were all but grown up now. Whitton had watched their progress over the past few months. They were no longer totally reliant on their parents – soon they would be off to start families of their own.

Laura shifted in Whitton's lap – she wanted to get a better view of the ducks. She chuckled as one of them, the male, surfaced and shook his head violently. Drops of water splashed his mate. Whitton kissed the baby on the top of her head and breathed in her scent. She couldn't get enough of the aroma her daughter gave off – a sweet, innocent aroma.

The ducks had decided to give up for the day and headed off to the other side of the lake. Whitton smiled. She thought about how her life had turned out.
"You know what," she said to Laura. "If somebody had come up to me two years ago and told me I'd be watching the ducks in the park with DS Jason Smith's little girl on my lap I'd have laughed until my jaws ached. Yet here we are."
Laura made a low gurgling sound by way of a reply.

Whitton took a bottle of formula milk from the pushchair next to them and handed it to Laura. The baby gripped it tightly and started to drink. She finished it in less than two minutes. Whitton picked her up and patted her on the back. Very soon, Laura expelled such a loud belch that a couple walking past couldn't help but smile.
Whitton smiled back at them. "She needs to work on her manners. She get's that from her Dad."

"I think it's time we made a move," Whitton picked up Laura and strapped her inside the pushchair. "Who knows what time your Daddy's coming home – he had to go back to work and you'll soon learn what that means."

She started to wheel the pushchair away from the lake when something caught her eye across the other side of the lake. The lake was small – roughly a hundred metres across. The sun was being reflected in something shiny and it was so bright that Whitton flinched. She looked across the lake and caught a glimpse of a large figure standing and hurrying off towards the exit of the park.

* * *

"Spot anything interesting?" Arnold Lewis asked the big man walking past him towards the exit gate.

"Excuse me?"

"Birds." Arnold pointed to the binoculars around the man's neck. "I caught a glimpse of a Great Crested Grebe the other week. Haven't seen it since, though."

"I'll look out for it," the big man said and hurried off down the path.

The woman was waiting for him on the road next to the park.

"Well?" she said when he got in the car.

"I'm not sure," he said. "I'm really not sure. The baby seemed so content."

"They all do. Don't let that fool you. You know what she is."

"Of course I know. But they seemed so happy."

"Grow a pair of balls. You owe me. This is all your fault. Remember what we talked about."

CHAPTER TEN

Frances King took a while to answer the door. Smith and Baldwin were about to give up when the door opened.

"I thought you'd want to speak to me," Frances said. "You'd better come in. Could I ask you to keep your voices down though – it took me ages to get the poor child off to sleep."

A noise from inside told Smith that Frances' efforts had been in vain. The child was screaming.

"We need to talk to him," Smith told Frances.

"Absolutely not."

"I know he's been through a lot, Mrs King," Baldwin chipped in. "But he may be the sole witness to the murder of his mother. He might have seen who did this. He might not be able to talk about it but we have to try."

Frances looked at Baldwin and then at Smith. "What's this? Good cop, bad cop?"

"It's my first day," Baldwin admitted. "I'm usually manning the front desk at the station. Please can we just try to speak with Jonathan? We'll try and make it as pleasant as possible under the circumstances."

"I don't think he really understands what's happened," Frances said. "How could he? He's only three and a half."

"Please, Mrs King," Smith said. "He might know who did this."

"His uncle is on the way," Frances said. "I think we ought to wait until he gets here. He should have some family around."

"You can stay with him when we speak to him," Baldwin said. "Please. We need to find out what happened."

Frances sighed. "I suppose it can't hurt. I'll go and get him."

Two minutes later Jonathan Collins sat on the carpet in Frances King's living room. A pad of paper and a set of crayons had been set out in front of him. He stared at PC Baldwin's uniform.

"Police," he said.

"Clever boy," Baldwin said to him. "We're both from the police. I'm a police constable." She pointed to Smith. "And he's a detective sergeant. Technically that means he's my boss."

Jonathan picked up a crayon and drew a single, straight line on the page.

"Can we have a chat with you?" she looked to Smith for approval.

Smith nodded to indicate she should carry on asking the questions.

"Jonathan," she said. "Can you remember what happened earlier today? You were at home with your Mummy. Is that right?"

"We had a fishes' finger."

Baldwin smiled. "Wow. I didn't even know fish had fingers. See, you're cleverer than I am. Was it just one fishes' finger? Or did you eat the whole fishes' hand?"

"Fishes don't have hands, silly." He drew three more lines on the paper. He'd drawn a crude rectangle. "They have fingles."

"Would you like some tea?" Frances asked.

"Coffee would be great," Smith replied. "Black, two sugars."

"Nothing for me, thanks," Baldwin said. She turned back to Jonathan. "What did you do after eating the fishes' finger?"

"Bed time, baby." He carried on drawing. The picture was taking shape. He'd now drawn another rectangle and four squares – he was drawing a picture of a house. "Bed time, baby."

"And your Mummy put you to bed."

"Bed time, baby."

"Laura has a nap after lunch, too," Smith told Baldwin.

Frances returned with a mug of coffee for Smith.

"So, Jonathan," Baldwin continued. "You went for your sleep after lunch. Was it a nice sleep?"

Jonathan nodded and carried on drawing. He was filling in the door of the house in black crayon.

"That's a nice house," Baldwin said. "Is that *your* house?"

There was a knock at the door and Frances got out of her chair. "That'll be Magda's brother."

She left the room and walked down the hallway.

"Jonathan," Smith said. "Do you remember how long you were asleep for?"

He wasn't expecting much but it was worth a try.

Jonathan shook his head.

"Where was your Mummy when you woke up?" Smith added.

The boy pointed to the door on his picture.

"I don't understand, Jonathan," Smith said.

"What the hell is going on here?" A short man with a huge beer belly came in. "What are you doing to my nephew?"

"What's that in the doorway?" Smith ignored him and put his finger where Jonathan had filled in the door with black crayon.

"I'm phoning my solicitor," Magda Collins' brother said. "You can't put a three and a half year old boy through this kind of interrogation."

"That's the man," Jonathan put his finger on Smith's.

"What man, Jonathan?"

"In the kitchen. He was bigger than the door."

CHAPTER ELEVEN

Smith ran out of Frances King's house and caught Grant Webber just in time. The head of forensics was about to drive away. Smith banged on the window and Webber rolled it down.
"What's wrong with you?" he said. "We've finished up at the Collins' place. If you don't mind, I'd quite like to get back to the lab. There's a lot we need to go over."
"You haven't finished," Smith panted. He was out of breath. "You need to check the garden at the back. The killer made his escape out through the kitchen door and into the back garden. The kid saw him in the doorway. Those size thirteen boot prints you found came from a very big bloke."

Smith followed Webber back inside Magda Collins' house. They headed straight for the kitchen. The first thing Smith did was roughly gauge the height of the door that led out to the garden. It appeared to be a standard size door.
"Check the handle for prints," he told Webber. "The door was closed when I got to the scene. If what Jonathan Collins had said was correct then the killer must have closed it behind him. "The outside handle especially. The kid saw the man in the doorway."
"Stay where you are until I'm finished," Webber ordered.
He donned a pair of gloves and pushed the door open. Smith watched him go outside. Webber wasn't tall – around five-nine. There was a good nine inches space between the top of his head and the top of the door frame. *This man must be at least six foot six*, Smith thought.

Webber reappeared in the doorway. "Come and have a look at this. Be careful, though – when you get outside, keep well to the left."
Smith went out and stepped to the left. The garden was well maintained. The grass was cut short and all the hedgerows appeared to have been well

looked after. The footprints on the grass were quite obvious – big footprints similar to the one Webber had found in the kitchen.

"He killed her by the door," Smith said. "He probably dragged her there so he could make a quick getaway. From the kid's drawing and the size of those boot prints I reckon he's incredibly strong. She wouldn't have stood a chance."

"She still might have put up a struggle," Webber said. "A mother being attacked with her child asleep nearby wouldn't go down without a fight."

"The path guys will find out." Smith walked to the left of the bloody boot prints. The red became more faded the more he walked towards the fence at the back of the garden. "He jumped over here." He stopped by the six foot fence. "We need to see what's behind it."

"It's an access road," Webber told him.

"He could've parked his car here earlier." Smith took hold of the top of the fence and pulled himself over.

He winced as something caught his arm on his way over. A nail was sticking out on the other side and it had scraped his forearm. A thin trickle of blood oozed out.

"Damn it." Smith looked around. The back of a row of garages ran the whole length of the access road on the opposite side to the Collins' back garden. There was nobody around. He walked down the road until he came to the end. Most of the gardens he walked past had huge trees in them – he was able to walk the whole length of the road unseen. He made his way back to the Collins' house and entered through the front door. Webber was still outside in the back garden.

"These people seem to like their privacy," Smith said. "You can jump over the fence and escape down the access road and nobody will be any the wiser."

"My guys are on their way back," Webber informed him. "We'll need to tape off the whole access road."

"Do you think you'll find anything?"

Webber frowned. "You should know by now, Smith – we always work on the assumption that we're going to find something. It's what keeps us all going. You included."

"It's getting late. I'll leave you to it. I'm calling a briefing in half an hour. Let me know if you find anything before that, will you?"

Smith's question didn't warrant an answer and Smith knew it. He left the head of forensics alone to do what he did best and went back outside to the street.

Baldwin was waiting outside the house next to Smith's car.

"We've got problems with Magda Collins' brother," she told him. "I tried to calm him down a bit but he's threatening us with his lawyer."

"Let him. It won't be the first time. Let's go. I'm calling a case meeting back at the station in half an hour."

"I hope I haven't got you into any trouble," Baldwin said as they drove back through the city to the station.

"Trouble?" Smith looked at her. "You were great back there – you're a natural. How did you learn to become a detective overnight?"

"Overnight? I *have* been paying attention these last few years. Do you think I want to be stuck behind that front desk for the rest of my life?"

"You won't be if I can help it. Even when Whitton comes back we'll still be a DC short. That is if Bridge or Yang Chu manage to pass the sergeants exam. I'm going to recommend you for my team. I can be quite persuasive when I have to be."

"I've noticed. Did you find anything in the Collins' back garden?"

"Just more bloody boot prints so far. Webber's team are on their way back. Whoever did this planned it very carefully. The access road at the back is pretty much hidden from the houses at the front and it's just a row of garages at the back. We'll do a door-to-door tomorrow to see if anybody saw anything but I'm not holding my breath. I want to go over what we've got so far before I think of how we're going to proceed with this one."

"I've always liked working with you."

"Don't speak too soon. It's still early days."

* * *

Half an hour later, Smith, Baldwin, Yang Chu, Bridge and Brownhill sat around the table in the small conference room.

"It's good to have you back, Sarge," Bridge said.

"I'll second that," Yang Chu added.

"OK," Brownhill said. "Before we get carried away with this sentimental crap, let's get to the matter in hand shall we? Smith, what have we got so far?"

"Not much," Smith admitted. "Julie Phelps was found by her neighbour at ten last night. Her six month old baby was screaming and that's what alerted the neighbour. She'd had her face smashed in with an iron of all things. There wasn't much left of it. I reckon whoever did this was very strong and they acted with quite a fury. The word, *UNWORTHY* was written on the window in blood. We've spoken to Mrs Phelps' husband and my gut is telling me he wasn't involved."

"I checked out his alibi," Yang Chu said. "At least two people can confirm he was in Newcastle from lunchtime yesterday until this morning when we called him about his wife."

"What else do we know about this Phelps woman?" Brownhill asked.

"She was a bit of a tart in her day," Yang Chu said.

"Yang Chu," Brownhill said. "Let's try to act with a modicum of professionalism shall we?"

"She was. She had quite a reputation by all accounts."

"We're still waiting for a list of her old acquaintances," Smith said.
"Apparently she used to knock around with some colourful characters before she met her husband."

"Did Grant have anything to give us?" Brownhill asked.

"Nothing yet," Smith replied. "He's still working on it. That brings me to the second murder. Magda Collins, thirty years old. Single mother of a three and a half year old boy. Her husband died last year from Cancer. Apparently he left her well provided for. It looks like she was stabbed with a carving knife. There was a lot of blood. We found the knife but Webber couldn't pull any prints from it. The word *Unworthy* was also carved in the fridge."

"Anything else?" Brownhill urged.

"Bloody boot prints. Size twelve or thirteen."

"That's big feet," Bridge joined in.

"And we have reason to believe our murderer is a very large man."

"How did you come to that conclusion?" Brownhill asked.

"We spoke to the boy."

"You interviewed a three and a half year old child?"

"His uncle wasn't too impressed," Smith admitted. "But Baldwin did a brilliant job. The boy told us the man was too big for the door – he had to be at least six foot six and wide with it."

"I don't like this," Brownhill said. "Please tell me there was somebody with the child when you spoke to him?"

"A neighbour," Baldwin said. "We didn't formally interview him – it was more of a friendly chat."

"Smith, if you ever pull a stunt like that again, I'll have you handing out parking tickets. Is that clear?"

"Crystal, boss. Right, does anybody have anything they want to say?" He looked around the room at the blank faces. "Anybody?" he urged.

"We need to find a connection between the two women," Brownhill broke the silence. "These were carefully planned murders. There has to be something that links them together."

"And why write the word, *Unworthy* at the scenes?" Baldwin said.

"What are these women unworthy of?" Brownhill asked.

"Both of them had small children," Bridge said. "Maybe whoever did this doesn't like kids."

"We'll look into it," Smith said. "Julie Phelps was in her mid-twenties. She appears to have led a colourful life before she got married. Her husband is ten years older than her. They married quickly when she found out she was pregnant. Magda Collins was thirty. No husband. She didn't want for much from the look of her house. What could possibly link them together?"

"And what could they have done that was so bad that someone would want to kill them with their children nearby?"

"There's one other thing I thought about," Baldwin said.

"Go on."

"Julie Phelps was alone in the house with her baby. Her husband was away at a reunion. I think the killer knew this. And if he did know, how?"

Brownhill smiled a rare smile. Baldwin noticed it and her face reddened.

"We'll look into that, too," Smith assured her.

"It's getting late," Brownhill said. "And I don't know about you but my brain is having trouble processing all this information. Let's call it a day. We'll make a fresh start in the morning with clear heads. We'll go through everything we have so far. Hopefully Grant will have something for us by then, too. Smith, before you go, I want a word with you. I'll see the rest of you at seven tomorrow morning."

Bridge didn't even try to hide his disgust. "Seven? Why so early?"

"Two women are dead, detective and it's our job to find out what happened to them."

"Seven it is then," Yang Chu agreed.

Bridge glared at him. They left the room together without saying a word.

"Baldwin," Brownhill said. "Could you wait outside until we're finished?"

"Before you start," Smith said to the DI when they were alone in the room. "It was my idea to talk to the Collins kid. Baldwin had nothing to do with it and he provided us with a description of the man. You have to admit, that's something at least."

"Smith, would you please shut up and let me speak. I've already spoken to you about that. I wanted to ask you how you thought Baldwin got on today. Do you think she's up to it? I've got a feeling that this one's not going to be easy. It's going to be one of those investigations that drags on."

"She's more than up to it. She impressed me today. We should've brought her on board years ago. It pains me to think of how long she's been wasted behind that front desk."

"It's still early days, but I'm inclined to agree with you. She can stay on the team but I'm going to be keeping a close eye on her."

"Me too, boss," Smith said. "I'll see you in the morning."

He left the conference room. Baldwin was standing outside. She looked extremely nervous. Smith gave her the thumbs up as he walked past.

CHAPTER TWELVE

Smith parked outside the Hog's Head and got out the car. He went inside the pub and breathed in the familiar scent of the place. It had been a while since he'd been there and he missed the smell of Marge's cooking. He walked up to the bar. Marge was replacing spirits on the optics at the back. Smith coughed and Marge turned round. She'd run the Hog's Head for as long as Smith could remember. It was one of only a few traditionally English pubs left in York and Marge was determined to keep it that way.
She smiled when she saw Smith standing there. "Jason, how are you? I haven't seen you for ages. How are you and Erica coping with the baby? She must be a couple of months old now."
"Six months. She's six months old and she's keeping us on our toes."
"How time flies. Pint?"
"Theakstons, please. And could you organise a couple of steak and ale pies to take away? It's been a long day and I don't feel like cooking. Whitton's probably knackered too."
"She does have a first name, you know. I'll see to that pint. Pies'll be about twenty minutes."
"Just enough time to finish the pint. Thanks, Marge."

Smith looked around the pub. It hadn't changed a bit since he was last there. He couldn't even remember when that was but it was a good few months ago.
Marge put the beer on the counter. "Penny for them?"
"Sorry, Marge."
"You were miles away there. Work?"
"Something like that." Smith took a long sip of the beer and then he took another one. "You'd better pour one more. I'd forgotten how good this stuff was."

Marge pulled another pint from the tap. "I'll get the pies done. Take away, you said?"

"Yes please. I'll be sitting by the window over there." He pointed to the table he always sat at when he was in the pub.

Smith finished his first beer and made a start on the second. He considered phoning Whitton to let her know he was bringing home a couple of pies but decided against it – he'd surprise her. His phone started to ring in his pocket. He took it out and looked at the screen – it was Baldwin. He answered it. "What's up, Baldwin?"

"Sorry to bother you, Sarge," Baldwin sounded agitated. "I can't stop thinking about the investigation. Has Webber come up with anything yet?"

"Not that I know of. We'll make an early start tomorrow. Until then, put it out of your head."

"Have you put it out of your head?"

"Until this phone call, I had actually. I'll see you tomorrow."

"One more thing, Sarge."

"Go on."

"The DI told me I'm officially on the team. I know I wouldn't be if it wasn't for you. I just want to say thank you."

"Don't thank me yet. Prove me right. Good evening, Baldwin." He rang off before she could say anything else.

* * *

Smith opened his front door and went inside. He found Whitton in the living room. She was asleep on the couch. Laura was sleeping on her lap. The TV was on. Smith kissed them both and took the pies through to the kitchen. He turned on the oven and took a beer out of the fridge. He took a long swig and went outside to the back garden for a smoke. He lit a cigarette and sat down on the bench. Even though it was starting to get dark it was still very warm.

"Rough day?" Whitton came outside and sat opposite him.

"Two brutal murders. These ones are particularly nasty."

Whitton picked up his beer and stole a swig. "Come on, then. Tell me all about it."

"Can we eat first? I picked up two of Marge's pies on the way home." He finished his cigarette and threw the butt over the fence into his next-door-neighbour's garden."

"Will you stop doing that?" Whitton said. She was finding it hard not to laugh.

"The grumpy old bastard needs something to moan about. Let's go and heat up those pies."

* * *

"Unworthy?" Whitton sat next to Smith on the sofa in the living room. A music DVD was playing – it was Joe Bonamassa live at the Albert hall. Laura was asleep in her cot upstairs.

"What do you think it means?" Whitton added.

"I have no idea," Smith admitted. "The first one was written in the woman's blood on the window and the second was carved into the fridge."

"It's definitely the same killer then?"

"Definitely. The word Unworthy aside, both victims were women with small children in the house when they were killed. One of the husbands was away and the other one is dead. I think our killer knew the women would be alone in the house with the children."

"Do you have anything to go on?"

"Not much. The second victim's three and a half year old might have seen the killer. He described him as too big for the door so I reckon we're looking at a big guy."

"That's something at least."

"That's if the kid's version is reliable – you know how imaginative children can be sometimes."

"How's Baldwin getting on?"

"We should have brought her on board years ago."

"I see," Whitton didn't sound too happy.

"What do you mean by that?"

"I've been replaced by the PC behind the front desk."

"I thought you liked Baldwin."

"I do. I do like her but I feel like an outsider stuck at home."

"Don't be silly."

Whitton turned up the volume on the TV. Joe Bonamassa was performing 'India, Mountain Time'. "So I'm being silly now?"

"Yes. And you haven't been replaced. You're ten times more experienced than Baldwin. I can't believe we're even having this conversation."

Whitton lay back on the sofa. "Are you sure I'm not being replaced?"

"Positive," Smith said. "You're irreplaceable."

Whitton slapped him on the shoulder.

"I mean it," Smith pulled her closer. "Besides, Bridge and Yang Chu are fighting it out for the DS position so we'll need another DC on the team anyway. Rather someone like Baldwin than an out-of-towner none of us know."

"How's the race to fill old Thompson's boots going?"

"Neck and neck at the moment. Bridge and Yang Chu aren't exactly on friendly terms right now."

"Who do you think will get it?"

"I don't know. Bridge has the most experience but he's his own worst enemy sometimes."

"Isn't that a prerequisite for a DS?"

Smith started to massage her shoulders. "But," he said. "Yang Chu is disciplined and he takes orders. It could go either way and they've both got the Sergeant's exam to get through first. Can we talk about something else now?"

"I don't feel like talking. That's nice."

Smith pressed his fingers harder on Whitton's shoulders. She put her hands on Smith's and moved them down to the waistband of her jeans.

"Erica Whitton," Smith said. "We have a baby girl upstairs."

"I know," she turned and kissed Smith's neck. "We won't disturb her down here."

CHAPTER THIRTEEN

Five miles away Joy Williams was celebrating. She didn't normally drink on a Tuesday night but the contract that was signed a few hours earlier warranted a celebratory drink or two after work. Joy sat in the Golden Hind pub in the city centre. With her, was her boss, Kenneth Love, Kenneth's wife Abigail and Fiona, Joy's PA.
"Another round?" Kenneth asked.
Joy looked at her watch. "I'd better not. It's getting late – I told the babysitter I'd be back by ten."
Kenneth opened his wallet and threw a ten pound note on the table. "Overtime. I'll pay. The babysitter will be glad of the extra cash. Same again?"

He returned with a tray of glasses and a bottle of Champagne. Two empty bottles of the same brand of Champagne already stood on the table. Kenneth popped the cork. "You know what this deal means don't you?" He poured four glasses. "It means we're growing stronger and stronger every day. Who would have thought it two years ago? Drink up. There's plenty more where that came from. We can put it on the expenses account – much better than the taxman getting his greasy hands on our hard-earned cash." Kenneth had started up an IT company a few years earlier. After struggling to keep up in the early days, his company had diversified and now they offered hi-tech security systems to large companies. Earlier that day they'd signed a contract with one of the largest chain stores in the country to provide CCTV and other security systems to all their retail outlets in the country. The monitoring of these systems could be done from one control centre in York and the running costs were minimal. Kenneth Love was set to become a very wealthy man overnight.

"I couldn't have done it without any of you," he raised his glass in the air. "And you will all benefit, I can promise you that."

Joy Williams looked at her watch again. It was 10:30. "I'd really better go. I still need to find a taxi and it'll take a good fifteen minutes to get home." She stood up before anybody could argue. "I'll see you in the morning."

"The rest of the week has been cancelled," Kenneth told her. "I think we've all earned a break after all the hard work we've put in over the last few weeks. You can enjoy an extra long weekend."

Joy was lucky. A taxi was parked across the pub when she got outside. "Turnbill Road," she said to the driver when she got in the back.

She was glad that the taxi driver wasn't one of those who felt he had to chat to pass the time – Joy hated small talk, and when she handed him the fare plus a tip and got out, she was feeling very pleased with herself. The new contract with the chain store meant a lot more money – she would probably be able to buy herself a new car, and it meant the worries of the last couple of years were finally over.

She turned the key in the lock of the front door. The door wasn't locked – the babysitter had forgotten to lock herself in.

How many times have I told that girl to lock the door when I leave? Joy thought but she wasn't in the mood for an argument. All she wanted to do was pay the babysitter and check on her eighteen month old daughter, Rose. She went through to the living room. The television was on – the volume was turned right down but the babysitter wasn't there.

"Katie," she said. "I'm home. Sorry I'm a bit late but the boss insisted."

No answer.

"Katie," she said again. "Where are you?"

She went upstairs.

Where is that girl? She thought. *Probably fallen asleep again. It wouldn't be the first time.*

Joy checked her daughter's room. Rose was fast asleep in her cot. There was still no sign of the babysitter. A terrible thought suddenly came to her. What if the babysitter had gone home already? What if she'd got tired of waiting and left Rose in the house by herself. Joy dismissed the thought straight away. Katie wouldn't do such a thing.

She kissed Rose on the forehead and walked along the landing to the bathroom. She was suddenly aware of a bad smell in the air – it was a mixture of BO and an odour she couldn't place. She opened the door to the bathroom and gasped. Katie, the babysitter was lying on the carpet. Her eyes were wide open and she had a nasty bruise on the side of her face. There was a rag stuffed in her mouth. Her legs were bound together with what looked like thick cable ties and her hands were behind her back.
"Oh my God," Joy moved closer to the terrified looking young girl. "What happened?"
Katie's eyes grew wider and Joy was aware of something in the doorway behind her. The room grew darker and she looked round.

The man had to stoop to get under the door frame. Joy looked back at the babysitter and turned to face the giant in her bathroom.
"What the hell are you doing in my house? Get out or I'll call the police."
The man didn't say anything. He held out his hands and Joy stepped back. He moved closer, put his hands round her neck and lifted her off the floor. Joy's legs kicked at him but his grip was relentless. She couldn't breathe. He held her in the air, all the time looking directly into her eyes. Joy tried to take in some air but it was no use. Her vision went black and then returned for a few seconds. She thought about the new contract Love IT had just signed then she thought about her daughter asleep in her cot a few metres away and then she felt nothing more.

CHAPTER FOURTEEN

The noise coming from downstairs woke Smith from a dreamless sleep. He shot up in bed. Laura was asleep in her cot but Whitton was nowhere to be seen. Smith got out of bed and looked at his daughter – she was smiling in her sleep. He went downstairs.

"Erica," he said.

There was an odd scraping noise coming from the kitchen.

"Erica," Smith said again. "What on earth are you doing?"

He walked through to the kitchen. Whitton wasn't there. The door to the fridge was open. Smith was about to close it when he spotted something at the back above a couple of beers. Something had been scraped into the ice box at the top. He took a closer look. The word *Unworthy* had been scraped deep into the plastic.

He raced to the living room. Whitton wasn't there either.

"Erica," he shouted.

He ran upstairs. He found her in the bathroom. She was lying on her stomach. A large knife was sticking out of her back.

"No!" he screamed and shot up in bed.

He was breathing heavily and he was covered in sweat. Whitton was lying next to him. His scream hadn't woken her. He took a few deep breaths and stroked her forehead. She didn't move. Her eyes were still, her mouth shut and she was extremely cold. Smith removed the duvet and saw the jagged wound in her chest.

"Jesus Christ!" Smith sat up in bed a second time.

This time Whitton woke with a start. "Bad dream?"

"It was another double awakening."

"I thought they'd stopped."

"So did I. I haven't had one since I found out I was going to be a Dad. That one really freaked me out."

A year or so earlier, Smith had been plagued by lucid dreams and double awakenings – they'd happened almost on a nightly basis and it was only through his sessions with Jessica Blakemore that the dreams had become less frequent and then finally stopped altogether. Jessica was a psychiatrist who'd been admitted to a psychiatric facility after a breakdown. She decided she preferred it in the hospital and as far as Smith was aware, she was still resident there.

Smith told Whitton about the dream.

"I wonder what's brought this on all of a sudden," Whitton said when he was finished.

"I have no idea. Jessica said the last ones were probably caused by my inability to disassociate myself from the investigation we were working on. She said I had difficulty switching off when I came home and the dreams were a way of letting me know."

"She's a nut job."

"She's not. She's just a bit disillusioned with the modern world. Who can blame her? She helped me last time."

"You're not going to go and see her again, are you?"

"Of course not. I'm sure that dream was just a once off."

Laura sat up in her cot and Whitton picked her up. "You don't have bad dreams, do you baby?"

"I'll make you a deal," Smith said. "You put the kettle on and make me the strongest cup of coffee possible and I'll see to this little stinker. What have you been feeding her? She smells worse than Theakston."

Whitton handed Smith his daughter. "Don't you listen to him. Nothing smells as bad as that dog."

Smith sat outside in the garden and lit a cigarette. The sun was up and it was already very warm. The dream had unsettled him. He wasn't sure what had caused it – he'd been involved in gruesome murder investigations before and the dreams hadn't occurred then so why were they happening again now?

Maybe it was just a once off, he thought. *Maybe I won't have any more.*
Whitton came out with two cups of coffee.

"What are your plans for today?" Smith asked her.

She put the coffees on the table, went back inside and returned with Laura.

"I thought we might drive out to the Moors. It's such a beautiful day. Laura's never been there before. We can take the dogs."

Theakston and Fred lollopped out and headed for the end of the garden.

"Now you're making me jealous." Smith took a sip of his coffee. "It ought to be quieter at this time of year."

"What about you?"

"Meeting, first thing. You know what it's like. Two women killed in the space of twenty four hours. The press are probably all over it already. Hopefully Webber has something for us. I don't like this one – I don't like it one little bit. When women are killed with their children nearby it's a bit too close to home for me. You keep your eyes and ears open. And lock the doors when you're inside."

"You don't have to worry about me. I can look after myself."

"That dream really freaked me out, that's all. I'd better go." He finished his coffee and kissed her and Laura on the cheek. "Have fun today. I'll call you to let you know what's going on."

* * *

Smith arrived at the station twenty minutes later. DCI Bob Chalmers arrived at the same time.

"Morning, boss," Smith said.

"I heard you'd come back early," Chalmers looked different – he'd shaved off his ridiculous moustache and Smith had to admit he looked much better for it. "How's fatherhood working out for you?" the DCI asked.

"I'm loving it. How's Smyth working out for *you*?"

Superintendant Jeremy Smyth was a bit of a laughing stock at the station. Nobody could really understand how the bungling ex-public school buffoon had ever reached the rank of Superintendent.

"I've got the measure of him," Chalmers took out a packet of cigarettes, lit one and handed the pack to Smith.

Smith took one and lit the end. "It took you long enough."

"Old Smyth's easy to manipulate," Chalmers explained. "You just have to put an idea in the idiot's head and convince him it's *his* idea. It's better that way. Are you making any progress on this Unworthy thing?"

"We don't have much," Smith admitted. "Two women killed with their kids nearby. Two different MO's and nothing so far to link them together."

"What about the husbands?"

Smith took a long drag of the cigarette and coughed. "One of the husbands was away at the time – his alibi checked out, and the other one's been dead for almost a year."

"What does your gut tell you?"

"Nothing, yet. We've got a meeting in..." He looked at his watch. "Ten minutes ago. Good to see you again, boss." He took a final drag on the cigarette and threw the butt into the distance.

"Sorry I'm a bit late." Smith walked in the conference room. Brownhill, Bridge, Yang Chu and Baldwin were already seated. "I was just catching up with the DCI."

"OK," Brownhill began. "Let's not waste any more time. Grant pulled an all-nighter on this one and we also have the path reports back for both women.

The boot prints found in the Collins' garden has been confirmed as a size 13. The blood on the prints belonged to Magda Collins."

"What about the writing on the window at Julie Phelps' place?" Smith asked. "Surely Webber could pull some good prints from that?"

"Yes. If the killer wasn't wearing gloves, that is. Grant's confirmed the smudge marks at the bottom of the letters are consistent with gloved fingers dipped in blood."

"No prints on the iron either, then?"

"Only Julie Phelps', I'm afraid."

"What about the path reports?" Baldwin asked.

"We'll get to those in due course. Julie Phelps' husband has come up with that list we asked him to compile – a list of Julie's former friends and acquaintances. It makes for interesting reading, I can tell you that."

"What do you mean?" Bridge said.

"At least half of them are quite well known to us."

"That's going to make things harder," Smith pointed out. "We need to prioritise that list."

Yang Chu looked puzzled. "Prioritise?"

"I assume a lot of the people on that list have criminal records?"

"That's right," Brownhill said.

"Then we need to go through them systematically. Leave out the petty stuff – house breaking and minor drug offences, and concentrate on those who've proven to be aggressive in the past. Both of these murders were particularly violent. We need to work through that list accordingly."

"Baldwin," Brownhill said. "I think that's right up your alley."

"I'll get on to it," Baldwin agreed. "What did the path reports give us?"

"Not much more than we already assumed from the scenes. Julie Phelps died from a number of blows to her face and head. Her skull was fractured in three places and there was also massive trauma to the brain. Brian Watson found her at around ten and from the reports, she hadn't been dead long before he found her."

"Whoever killed her hadn't long left when the Watson bloke found the body," Smith said. "He was lucky."

"Yes," Brownhill said. "That poor baby was screaming his head off for hours. He was screaming while his mother was being killed."

"Why didn't the killer just shut the kid up?" Bridge asked. "It was very risky to let him carry on screaming the whole time."

"The baby wasn't who he wanted to kill," Smith said. "It's quite clear that it's the mothers this maniac is targeting."

"But why?" Yang Chu asked. "What would make someone want to go to so much trouble to kill two mothers?"

Smith thought about the dream he'd had. Jessica Blakemore had told him that double-awakenings were extremely rare and the lucid types were experienced by a very small percentage of the population. She'd suggested that the nightmares could be caused by extreme moments of stress or severe trauma. Another theory was that they indicated a certain psychosis in the sufferer. Smith had dismissed that theory as soon as the words had left the psychiatrist's lips.

"Are you still with us?" Brownhill asked.

"Sorry," Smith blinked hard. "I was just thinking of something. What about the path report for the other woman?"

"Magda Collins. Mrs Collins died from a knife wound to the heart. There were six other stab wounds but it was the one that pierced her heart that killed her."

"Time of death?"

"Sometime between noon and 1pm yesterday."

"He was taking a chance killing her during the day," Bridge pointed out.

"He came in through the back and left the same way," Smith said. "The road at the back of the house is quiet and the trees in most of the back gardens mean he could come and go unseen. I think he planned it quite carefully. He could have parked a car there and nobody would even think twice about it."

"Right," Brownhill's tone told everybody that she was wrapping the meeting up. "This is how we're going to play it. Baldwin, you can go through that list of Julie Phelps' old delinquent friends – Bridge, you and Yang Chu are to speak with the Collins' neighbours. It's a long shot but someone might have seen something – a car parked near the house they didn't recognise for instance."

"I've got an idea," Smith said.

"Go on."

Smith was still thinking about his nightmare. He'd come up with an idea to kill two birds with one stone. "I want to go and see Jessica Blakemore."

"Absolutely not," Brownhill said.

"She's a total whack-job," Bridge added.

"Hear me out," Smith said.

"No," Brownhill was adamant. "Jessica is sick. She'll admit it herself. I'll not have you wasting your time on a dead end. I want you to do some digging around in Magda Collins' life. Find out more about her. Speak to everybody who knew her – family, friends and the like. I have a meeting with the Super I can't get out of. We'll meet back here at three this afternoon to go over what we find out."

CHAPTER FIFTEEN

DI Brownhill's words still rang in Smith's head as he left the city behind and turned left onto the road that led to the Lemonwood Psychiatric Hospital. The imposing walls of Full Sutton Prison could be seen far in the distance. The prison's close proximity to the peaceful hospital grounds had always seemed wrong to Smith. He didn't really know why. He parked his car in the parking area and got out.

What am I doing here? he lit a cigarette and turned to face the sun. Brownhill had made it clear he was not to visit Jessica Blakemore. Smith realised he didn't even know if she was still here. It had been over a year since he'd last visited her – maybe she'd got better and been discharged. "Only one way to find out," he said out loud and finished his cigarette.

The reception area in the hospital had changed. It had obviously had a new lick of paint recently. The drab light brown had been replaced with a bright yellow and the window frames had been painted green. The woman Smith met behind the desk was also new. Joe, the familiar face who'd always greeted Smith before was nowhere to be seen.

"Morning," Smith said. "Is Joe not in today?"

"Joe left nine months ago," the woman said. "Can I help you?"

Smith had to think hard about how he was going to play it. Joe had always let him visit Jessica without question but Smith could tell from the expression on the face of this new receptionist, this wasn't going to be easy.

"I'm here to see Jessica. Jessica Blakemore."

"Visiting time isn't for another hour. You'll have to come back then."

"So Jessica is still here then?"

"You're the one who's here to see her. Surely you know whether she's here or not?"

"Sorry," Smith decided to tell her the truth. "My name's Jason Smith. I'm a detective sergeant with the York police department. I haven't been to see her for a while. Jessica has helped us out with a number of cases in the past."

"Has this been authorised?"

"Authorised?"

"Mrs Blakemore is a patient here. You can't just walk in here and expect her to help you without some kind of permission."

This was going to be harder than Smith thought.

"What if we ask her? Ask her if she wants to talk to me."

The woman rolled her eyes and picked up the telephone. "Dr Grace. There's a DS Smith here from York. He's asking to speak to Jessica." She listened for a while. "OK. I'll let him know." She replaced the handset. "You can go through," she said to Smith. "I assume you still remember the way?"

Smith set off down the corridor without saying another word to the dour receptionist. He wondered where Joe had ended up – he'd always been courteous and helpful when Smith visited. He stopped outside Jessica's room and knocked. She opened it immediately.

"DS Jason Smith," she smiled at him. She'd changed dramatically since Smith's last visit. The hair she'd shaved off had grown back and she had a rosy complexion. "I assume you're still a DS? What can I do for York's worst lost-cause?"

"Nice to see you too. I'm sorry to barge in unannounced."

"When did you ever make an appointment? Let's go outside. Last I heard, the sun was out."

They walked past the day room and out through the courtyard to the lawn outside. The smell of freshly cut grass lingered in the air and Smith breathed in deeply. A row of wooden benches had been put down on the lawn. Jessica chose the one furthest away from the building.

"I heard you and DC Whitton had a baby together," she said and sat down. Smith sat opposite her. "Laura – she's six months old now."

"And how's that all going? Are you having problems? Is that why you're here? I'm not a marriage guidance counselor you know."

"No, you're not. I need your advice about something else altogether."

"Are you still having the dreams?"

"I had one last night. It's the first one I've had since I found out Erica was pregnant. I want to ask your opinion about something else first."

"Shoot. I charge by the hour now, though."

"Two women were brutally killed. One at around ten the night before last and another yesterday afternoon. The first one had a six month old boy and the second, a three and a half year old. Both kids were present when their mothers were killed."

"That's awful. What do you think I can tell you about it?"

"I'm not finished. We're certain it was the same killer. The word *Unworthy* was written at both of the murder scenes – first in blood on the window in the living room and then scratched into the fridge in the kitchen."

"Unworthy?"

"That's right."

"And what do you think it means?"

"We've chucked a few theories around and the most obvious one is whoever killed these women believed them to be unworthy of something."

Smith's phone started to ring in his pocket. He took it out and saw it was DI Brownhill. He let it go straight to voicemail.

"Sorry," he said. "Where was I?"

"Unworthy," Jessica said. "You were about to explain your theory."

"What these two women were unworthy of is still a mystery. The first one had a bit of a colourful past – she had a reputation for dropping her knickers at the drop of a hat but the second victim was a reasonably upstanding citizen as far as we're aware. There's nothing to connect them together beside the fact that they both had a young child."

"What about the fathers?"

"One was away when his wife was killed and the other died last year."

"Mmm. You haven't given me much to go on. What else can you tell me?"

"The three and a half year old reckons he saw a man in the doorway after his mother was killed – a very large man. The rest of the team are busy talking to the neighbours and going through a list of the first victim's old acquaintances."

"While you're here putting your faith in a whack-job shrink? Why do you always seem to end up here, Jason?"

"I like the view."

"Do you want to know what I think? I think you're scared."

"I'm not scared."

"The dream you had last night – it was a double awakening wasn't it?"

"I already told you that."

"No you didn't. You said you'd had a dream. It's quite simple to explain. You're a father now – your priorities have changed. You have an overwhelming instinct to protect your baby – this little part of you. Did the dream involve Whitton being killed?"

"It did."

"And the baby was left unharmed?"

"Yes."

"It's starting all over again. I'm actually getting tired of repeating myself. You're unable to differentiate between work and home and until you learn how to do that, there's nothing more I can do for you."

Smith lit a cigarette. "Can you help me with the investigation or not?"

Jessica looked at the smoke oozing out of his nose. "How were the women killed?"

"The first one had her face smashed in with an iron – there wasn't much left of it after he'd finished."

"And the second woman?"

"She was stabbed repeatedly. Her heart was pierced."

"You said after *he'd* finished."

"Did I?"

"You did. What makes you think a man did this?"

"The young boy described a man in the doorway. We also found large boot prints at the scene – size thirteen. How many women do you know with feet that big?"

"The killer leaves a message for someone to find – *Unworthy.* That seems to me more like something a woman would think up."

"So you think a woman did this?"

"I don't think anything yet. You haven't given me much to go on but from what you have told me, yes, I think a woman is more likely to kill another woman and leave that kind of calling card behind. It just doesn't sound like something a man would come up with. Nobody knows you're here do they?"

"Not exactly."

"I'll tell you what I'll do," Jessica seemed to be thinking hard. Her suntanned brow was creased up. "Let me give it some thought. Like I said, you haven't given me much to go on but I'll see what I can come up with. I assume your mobile number is still the same?"

"It is."

"Then let me see what jumps out at me."

"Thank you, Jessica. You're looking well. Surely you don't need to be in this place anymore. There's nothing wrong with you as far as I can see."

"And, as you're the one asking a nut-job for psychiatric advice, I'll take that with a pinch of salt. I'll be in touch, Jason."

CHAPTER SIXTEEN

TWENTY YEARS EARLIER

"You don't go too far now," the mother of the two children told them. "And stick together, you hear me?"
The boy was twelve, his sister exactly a year and one day older.
"Make sure you're back before it gets dark," their mother called after them but she wasn't sure if they could still hear her.

"Where are we going, Bee?" the boy asked. "I want to go to the beck."
"We'll go to the beck afterwards," his sister assured him. "And stop calling me Bee. You're not five anymore."
"Bee, Bee, Bee," he said and ran ahead of her.
He was much faster than her now. And much, much stronger. Their mother was surprised at how much he'd grown in such a short space of time. He was twelve years old and already an inch short of six feet.

Two older boys approached from the opposite direction. The girl known to her brother as Bee knew them well – too well, and her heart started to beat faster. These boys were trouble. Trouble ran through their veins.
"Let's cross over the road," she said to her brother.
"What for?"
"Just do it." She started to walk across.
The two boys did the same so she crossed back. Her brother realised what was going on and stepped in front of her.
"Where you going?" the taller of the two boys looked past Bee's brother and spoke directly to his sister. "We've got some beers if you're interested."
"I don't drink," she told him. "Leave us alone."
"Yes. Leave us alone," her brother said.

He was at least two inches taller than the boy and his height seemed to do the trick.

"Come on, Wayne," the boy said to his friend. "These two are chicken, anyway."

Bee felt a surge of relief rush through her as they carried on walking down the road.

"The becks full, Bee," the boy exclaimed as they made their way through the trees and emerged onto the other side.

It had rained heavily in the past few days and the river that ran into the beck had filled it to the brim. The beck was no more than a small pool – about ten metres in diameter. But it was deep. During the summer months children flocked here and the braver ones swam in the water. It was late September now and Bee and her brother had the place to themselves.

"I'm going to climb up there," Bee's brother pointed to a sturdy tree. Its branches hung over the edge of the beck.

"You be careful," Bee warned. "I'm just going to lie here in the sun for a bit." She walked to the edge of the beck - there was a place where the sun had made its way through the trees. She brushed some dirt away from the rocks and lay on her back.

Her brother started to make his way up the tree. It had been a while since he'd climbed this particular tree and he was surprised at how hard it had become – he'd grown quite a bit since the last time and his long legs kept getting caught in the branches. He made his way up regardless and looked down at his sister. She was on her back on the rocks six or seven metres below. It looked like she was sleeping.

Bee wasn't sleeping. She had her eyes closed and she was enjoying the sunshine while it lasted. Very soon, Autumn would come, the nights would last longer and sunshine would be hard to find. Bee was thinking about Christmas – it wasn't too far away when she thought about it. Less than three months. She loved Christmas. She had wanted a saxophone for quite some time – she'd dropped hints whenever she could and the feeling she got from her parents was positive. She would get her saxophone this Christmas.

Her brother was making slow progress up the tree. He was simply too large now to be able to climb it like he used to. He stopped on one of the branches over the beck. He tested it with his leg first to make sure it was strong enough. He stood up to grab onto a higher limb so he could pull himself up, there was a loud crack and the branch he was standing on came apart from the trunk of the tree.

Bee heard the crack and opened her eyes. She caught a brief glimpse of her brother hanging onto the tree above her and then the huge branch hit her on the waistband of her jeans.

CHAPTER SEVENTEEN

"Have you heard anything from Smith?" DI Brownhill asked Baldwin in the canteen.
Baldwin was taking a well-earned break from going through the list of Julie Phelps' old acquaintances. She'd been working non-stop for the past three hours.
"I've been stuck in Smith's office going through that list," she said. "I'm just grabbing a cup of coffee. I thought he was out trying to find out more about Magda Collins."
"He's not answering his phone."
"He's probably just busy with something."
"It's that something I'm worried about. I hope he hasn't gone to see Jessica Blakemore at the hospital."
"Why would he do that?"
"I saw that look on his face."
"What look?"
"It was *that* look. When Smith get's something into his head he doesn't let it lie."

"I assume you're talking about me," Smith sat down opposite Brownhill.
"Where have you been?" the DI asked. "I tried to call you."
"Flat tyre. I had my hands full with the spare and the wheel spanner. What's up?"
"What did you find out about Magda Collins?"
"Not much." Smith had spoken again with the neighbour, Frances King. He'd gone there straight from the hospital. Magda Collins' brother was still there.
"The little boy is going to stay with Magda's brother, James for the time being. Poor kid – the man's a real moron."
"He's just lost his sister," Baldwin pointed out.

"He's still a moron. He's still talking about suing us for interviewing the kid without permission. *Interrogating* was the word he used."

"What could he tell you about his sister?"

"Like I said, not much. She didn't have any enemies as far as he knew – she pretty much kept herself to herself after her husband died."

"What about insurance policies?" Baldwin asked. "I believe she was pretty loaded. Shouldn't we find out who stands to gain now she's dead?"

"All in good time," Brownhill said. "The estate will probably go into a trust for the child. That's how it usually works. We'll check anyway."

"Did you get much from the list of Julie Phelps' reprobate friends?" Smith asked Baldwin.

"A motley crew," Baldwin replied. "I've organised the list like this : Those with tendencies towards violence are at the top followed by the nasty-pieces-of-works and the petty crims are at the bottom."

"And how many violent ones have we got?"

"Three. Two did time for GBH and the other one was in for attempted murder. She only got out six months ago."

"She?" Brownhill said.

"Mary Quinn. 36 years old. She beat a teenager to an inch of his life with a baseball bat. She served 10 years."

"And the GBH's?"

"Two brothers. Kenneth and Scott McFarlane. They were both sent down at the same time for a vicious assault on a bouncer at one of the clubs in the city centre. Kenneth got 3 years and his brother, 4. I've spoken to the parole officers of the both brothers and Mrs Quinn. The McFarlanes seem to have kept their noses clean since they got out."

"And Mary Quinn?"

"That's the strange part. Our Mrs Quinn appears to have disappeared into thin air."

* * *

Smith stopped outside the address he'd been given for Mary Quinn and turned off the engine. Mary's parole officer had informed him that he'd tried to contact Mary on several occasions to no avail. He'd made numerous phone calls and called round to the house five times. Mary had disappeared.

"Nobody just disappears," Smith said to Baldwin as they walked up the path to the house.

"Maybe she's just moved," Baldwin suggested.

"Then she ought to have informed her parole officer."

He knocked on the door and waited. Nothing. He knocked on the door again and peered through the letterbox. A pile of correspondence covered the carpet behind the door. He tried the door handle but it was locked.

"It looks like she hasn't been here for a while."

"What are we going to do?"

"Nobody's seen or heard from her for ages. Let's have a look inside, shall we?"

"I'll see if I can get the details of the landlord."

"That'll take too long. Stand back." He turned away and smashed one of the glass panels in the door with his elbow.

He removed the remaining glass from the frame, put his hand inside and opened up the door.

"I don't think we're actually allowed to do this, sir," Baldwin said.

"We're looking for a woman who may know something about two recent murders. Her parole officer has reported that he hasn't seen or heard of her for a while. She's therefore in violation of her parole terms and we have the right to apprehend her."

Baldwin kept quiet.

"Anyway," Smith continued. "Something might have happened to her. She could be lying dead inside the house for all we know."

Mary Quinn wasn't lying dead in her house. After a thorough search, Smith realised she'd gone. The house was empty – everything that could be removed had been removed, including many of the light fittings and electrical sockets.

"She didn't leave much behind," Baldwin noted.

"No," Smith was rummaging through the letters and junk mail on the carpet by the front door. "Maybe there's something here that can give us a clue to where she went." He looked through the mail. "Looks like mostly bills and final reminders. She's wasn't exactly an ideal tenant by the looks of these."

"What do we do now?"

"Take this lot with us and put the word out."

"Do you think she's our *Unworthy* killer? I thought we were looking for a man. Jonathan Collins described a man in the doorway."

"Let's not rule anything out yet. It could be a woman. It's just something that Jessica Blakemore..."

"You went to see her didn't you? You went to see her after the DI made it clear you weren't to go there?"

"I might have popped in for a short chat. Anyway, Jessica said something that makes sense the more I think about it. *Unworthy* is more like something a woman scorned would write."

Smith's phone started to ring.

He answered it. "Smith." It was Brownhill.

"We've found her," the DI said. "Mary Quinn. Her parole officer phoned. She's been in Spain for the past week. On holiday. She moved out of her old place before she left and now she's living in a Council place on the Greenford Estate."

"I know it. What's the address?"

"No need. She got hold of her parole guy and he instructed her to show her face at the station. The parole officer is on his way."

CHAPTER EIGHTEEN

Mary Quinn was waiting in Interview Room 2. Brownhill wanted to sit in on the interview with Smith and it took him a while to persuade the DI that Baldwin needed the experience.
"She's learning fast," Smith explained. "But I want her to be involved in all aspects of this investigation. She needs to do this."
Brownhill didn't seem too convinced. "I've dealt with the likes of Mary Quinn before – she's a hardened criminal and I don't think Baldwin can handle it just yet."
"She can handle it. Just give her a chance to prove herself."
"What's with you and Baldwin? You appear to be taking a rather keen interest in her."
"I think she's got what it takes to be a good detective, that's all. Trust me."

Five minutes later, Smith and Baldwin sat opposite the 'hardened criminal.' Mary Quinn didn't look like the archetypal hardened criminal – she looked younger than her 34 years and the tan and the sparkle in her eyes didn't suggest she'd recently spent ten years behind bars. Her hair was brown and bleached blonde in places and she wore jeans and a T-Shirt that showed off her recently acquired tan.
"Interview with Mary Quinn commenced 11:45," Smith began. "Present – DS Smith and PC Baldwin." Smith looked across at Mary. "Mrs Jones. Thank you for coming in. You do realise that leaving the country without informing the relevant authorities is a direct violation of your parole terms?"
Mary smiled. "It was an offer I couldn't resist. I didn't think a week away would cause too much bother."
"You can plead that matter with your parole officer. We'd like to talk to you about something else."

Smith knew that since she'd been abroad while the two murders were carried out, she had perfect alibis for both.

"Mrs Quinn, how well did you know Julie Phelps?"

"I knew her when she was Julie Pratt. I must admit, Julie Phelps sounds much better than Julie Pratt don't it?"

"I assume you've heard what happened to Julie?"

"I read it in the paper. She should never have married that toff."

"Toff?"

"John. I can't stand the man. Thinks he's much better than the rest of us. Julie thought she were going up in the world but she went right down in my opinion."

"How do you mean?"

"We was alright for her before she met him but afterwards, she started acting all posh. It's pathetic."

"Julie was murdered, Mrs Quinn," Baldwin joined in. "Doesn't that bother you at all?"

Mary looked at Baldwin as though she was looking at a dog turd. "You spend ten years inside and not much bothers you anymore, love. Look, I'm sorry that she's dead – I wouldn't wish that on anyone but it don't bother me too much, no."

"OK," Smith decided on a change of tack. "Can you think of anybody who might have wanted to hurt Julie?"

"No."

"Think. What about after she married John Phelps? You said yourself that you weren't too happy about it. Was there anyone else who might have borne a grudge? An old boyfriend, perhaps?"

Mary started to laugh. "Boyfriend? How long have you got? Julie had more boyfriends than anybody I've ever met. I couldn't believe it when she said she was settling down with that twit. I wouldn't be surprised if the kid isn't his though."

"So nothing springs to mind? You can't think of anyone who would want to hurt Julie?"

"I told you, no."

"You were found guilty of attempted murder," Baldwin said. "What happened?"

Mary folded her arms across her chest. "I'd do it again if I had to."

"What happened?" Smith asked. "I believe you assaulted a young man with a baseball bat."

"Vincent Stewart. Real little bastard. Him and his gang were going around terrorizing the estate. Thought he was the dog's bollocks he did. Well, my late dad always said 'go for the main man and the rest'll crumble like sand,' so that's what I did. They was hassling a couple just outside the place I lived at the time. Six of them against this middle-aged couple. I went inside, got me baseball bat and went to sort them out. I still remember the smug grin on the little scrote's face. 'Whatya going to do with that, Mary?' he said. I went straight past his mates and whacked him one on the side of the head. I gave him a couple more for good measure. They say I fractured his skull, broke a couple of ribs and shattered his knee cap. The rest of the gang ran off in all directions. Real brave ones."

"And you got ten years for attempted murder?" Baldwin said. "Surely you could have argued self defence? Didn't the couple you were protecting stand up for you in court?"

Mary looked at Smith. "Is she for real?" she glanced over at Baldwin. "Nobody stands up for nobody these days. I did and look where it got me. I couldn't afford some fancy solicitor so I went down for ten years. I did my time and I don't want any more trouble. Vincent Stewart don't walk too well these days – that's one good thing that came out of it. Can I go now?"

Smith couldn't see any point in keeping her any longer. "Interview with Mary Quinn finished 12:25." He switched off the machine. "You're free to go. If you think of anything else, please give me a call." He handed her one of his cards.

"Do you think I'll have to go back inside for the parole violation?"

"I doubt it. You'll probably get off with a warning."

* * *

"She's more of a hero in my eyes," Baldwin said in the canteen. "I can't believe she got ten years for sticking up for someone."

"She almost killed the kid with a baseball bat," Smith pointed out. "You can't go around doing stuff like that – however much the kid deserved it. Besides, she neglected to mention the other things she was mixed up in at the time. She was hardly squeaky clean."

Baldwin took a sip of her coffee and winced. "This tastes off to me. Anyway, she didn't give us much to go on with the Julie Phelps killing."

"No," Smith agreed. "I'm starting to think we need to look more closely at Julie Phelps' life after she left her friends behind and married John Phelps."

"There has to be a connection between Julie and Magda Collins, too."

"I agree. I don't believe these two women were selected at random – something must link them together."

Yang Chu and Bridge walked in together. Bridge headed straight for the coffee machine in the corner. Yang Chu sat down opposite Baldwin. He looked exhausted.

"Find anything from the neighbours?" Smith asked him.

"Sod all. Most of them were at work the time the murder took place. That estate is mostly middle class sorts. We did think we were getting close at one stage – a retired bloke thinks he could have seen a blue car parked in the access road at around lunch time but he's not sure."

Bridge sat down. "I thought old people were supposed to be observant – I mean they've got bugger all to do all day, but this guy wasn't sure if it was a Ford or a Vauxhall. Christ, he's not even certain if it was parked there yesterday or the day before. That was a complete waste of time."

"Ninety percent of our time is wasted," Smith said. "You should know that by now."

"I can't wait until I'm a DS," Bridge added. "At least then I'll get paid more for having my time wasted."

"You'll have to go through me first," Yang Chu said.

"Bring it on. They always give it to the one with the most experience and right here, right now, that's me, mate." He nodded to Smith. "Isn't that right, Sarge?"

"You'll be selected on merit," Smith told him. "You still have to pass the sergeants exam first."

"He's got no chance," Yang Chu scoffed. "He'd rather be out pissing it up than swotting for a test. He thinks being a DS means you have to be able to hold your drink."

Smith was starting to get annoyed at the constant bickering between the two DC's. "That's enough, you two. We need to put all our efforts into this investigation. Baldwin and me drew a blank with the list Julie Phelps' husband gave us. The odds-on favourite was out of the country when the murders occurred. And nobody I spoke to who knew Magda Collins could think of any reason why anybody would want to harm her."

"So what do we do now, Sarge?" Bridge asked.

"Motive, Bridge. That's what we do now but first we need to find a connection between these two women. There has to be something. These weren't random murders - something made these women stand out. Something links them both together. Once we find out what that is, we can start looking in the right direction."

CHAPTER NINETEEN

DCI Bob Chalmers came in the room. From the expression on his face, everyone could tell he wasn't in the best of moods.
"We've got a bit of a situation," he said. "James France, Magda Collins' brother has laid an official charge against us." He looked directly at Smith. "With you in particular. Old Smyth is taking it very seriously. What is it with you, Smith? You've been back at work for five minutes and you're already causing shit."
"What's the charge?" Smith asked him.
"You interviewed a three and a half year old boy without a parent or guardian present."
"We didn't interview him. We had a chat with him. He gave us some useful information. Besides, the neighbour sat in while we spoke to the kid."
"That's neither here nor there. The Super wants to see you." He tapped Baldwin on the shoulder. "You too."

* * *

Superintendant Jeremy Smyth was staring out the window in his office when Smith and Baldwin arrived. Some awful music was coming out of an MP3 player on his desk and Smyth was swaying from side to side. Baldwin chuckled and Smith shook his head.
"Afternoon, sir," Smith shouted and Smyth jumped.
He turned the volume down on the MP3 player.
"Nice music," Smith said. "I've always meant to get round to listening to more Michael Bolton."
"Yes, he does have a rather unique twang to his voice," Smyth said. His face broke into a frown. "Please take a seat. I'm afraid this business isn't going to go away."
Smith and Baldwin sat at the desk opposite the Superintendant.

"Mr France isn't backing down," Smyth continued. "And interviewing a minor without a parent or guardian present is a very serious violation of one's rights. I'm sure you appreciate that."

"With all the respect in the world due to you, sir," Smith said. "We didn't interview the kid. Me and Baldwin had a quiet chat with him and he gave us something concrete to go on. He may have seen the man who killed his mother."

"I see," Smyth scratched at a scab on his chin. "I've tried to smooth things over but Mr France is quite adamant. His lawyer has set the ball in motion."

"What the hell does that mean?" Smith said much louder than he intended.

"It means there will be a full internal investigation. And I'd appreciate it if you'd watch your tone in here."

"Sorry, sir. Two women have been killed in the space of a couple of days. We're positive it was the same killer. I appreciate that Mr France is hurting over the death of his sister but an internal investigation right now isn't going to help catch his sister's killer."

"What can we do to make this right?" Baldwin asked.

Smyth sighed. "I'm afraid it's too late for that. I have no option but to suspend you both pending the outcome of the internal investigation."

"We have a slightly more important external investigation going on at the moment, sir," Smith argued. "Surely our priority is to catch the bastard who killed those women?"

"I'll ask you once again to watch your tone in here, detective. You're entitled to the representation of a union rep. I suggest you make use of that right."

"Surely there's another way around this?" Baldwin said. "I can't afford to have a suspension on my record at this point in my career."

"You should have thought about that when you ignored protocol and interviewed the boy. You'll be informed in due course as to the outcome but in the meantime you're no longer part of the ongoing investigation."

Smith stood up before he said something that might lead to something worse than a mere suspension. "Come on, Baldwin, the Super's right. We'll just have to wait for the outcome of the internal."

"Are you feeling alright, Sarge?" Baldwin asked Smith outside in the car park.

"What do you mean?"

"I can't believe you took that lying down. You let the Super walk all over you back there. I seem to remember not so long ago you would've at least mentioned something derogatory about his public school education."

"You learn after a while how to handle people like old Smyth. Let's go."

"Where are we going?"

"To see if I can break my record for the shortest suspension ever. It stands at two days. We're going to speak to James France. I'm sure between the two of us we can make him withdraw the charges against us."

* * *

James France didn't seem especially pleased to see Smith and Baldwin standing on the doorstep of his sister's house.

"I've got nothing to say to you. Everything that needs to be discussed can go via my lawyer."

He closed the door but Smith was too quick – he jammed his foot in the gap.

"Mr France. Please can you just give us five minutes of your time? Listen to what we have to say. If you still want to continue with the charges against us after we've spoken, we won't try and stop you."

"Please, Mr France," Baldwin joined in.

"Five minutes," France opened the door. "Jonathan's asleep so could you please keep your voices down?"

He led them through to the living room. "I won't offer you anything to drink if that's alright with you."

"This won't take long," Smith sat down in a leather armchair. "I realise what this might look like to you – talking to Jonathan without asking you first, but we had no choice. The boy might have seen who killed his mother. He spoke of a very large man in the doorway."

"That still doesn't excuse your lack of protocol, not to mention common decency. Jonathan's mother has just been killed – the last thing the poor child needs is to be interrogated by the police. It could scar him for life."

"Mr France," Baldwin said softly. "We're sorry for yours and Jonathan's loss but we need to find out who did this. We're extremely short-staffed at the moment and should myself and DS Smith be suspended that will only draw out the investigation even more and none of us want that do we? I'm sure you'll agree that we all want the same thing here – we want whoever is responsible for this to be stopped and punished."

The room was silent for a while. A wasp was trying to get out the window on the far side of the room. Its frustration could be heard quite clearly. Each time it reached the top of the window and dropped back down, its buzzing became more high-pitched.

"I'm not saying I agree with your methods," James France said eventually. "But of course I want Magda's killer caught." He looked Smith in the eye. "Do you think you'll catch him?"

"Yes," Smith said straight away. "We'll catch him."

"I'll speak to my lawyer. I'll explain I was a bit hasty and try and get the charges dropped."

"Thank you, Mr France," Smith said. "It's getting late. We'll probably need to speak to you and Jonathan again but we'll arrange that for a more convenient time. We won't take up any more of your time."

CHAPTER TWENTY

"Do you think it worked?" Baldwin asked Smith outside Magda Collins' house.

"We'll find out tomorrow. As of now, we're still officially suspended. Do you feel like a drink?"

"I'd better not."

"Why not?"

"Shouldn't you be getting back to Whitton and the baby?"

"Just a quick drink. We'll drink to being partners in crime. I've never been suspended with someone by my side before. It's quite refreshing."

"I suppose one drink won't hurt. Could you drop me off at home first though? I need to get this uniform off."

"No problem. And if our friend Mr France does what he says he's going to do, I'd say you can lose the uniform while you're working on this investigation."

* * *

The Hog's Head was quiet when Smith and Baldwin walked in. Marge was sitting with an elderly man at one of the tables. She frowned when she spotted Smith and Baldwin.

"Evening, Marge," Smith said. "Could I get a pint of Theakstons please? What are you having?" He asked Baldwin.

"I'll have the same?" Baldwin replied.

"Coming up," Marge stood up and went to pour the drinks.

"This is PC Baldwin," Smith told Marge by the bar. "She's helping us out for a while."

Marge looked Baldwin up and down. "Pleased to meet you. Will there be anything else?" she asked Smith. "Perhaps a takeaway for Erica?"

"No thanks, Marge," Smith said. "We're just having a quick drink after work. It's been an exhausting day."

Marge put the beers on the counter.

"I need to use the Ladies," Baldwin said.

"Through there on the right," Smith pointed to the corridor that ran next to the bar.

"She's pretty," Marge said when Baldwin was gone.

Smith took a long sip of his beer and wiped his mouth. "Is she?"

"I hope you know what you're doing."

"What do you mean?"

"You've got a child at home, Jason," Marge said and Smith winced.

She emphasised his first name as if she wanted to get some kind of point across.

"And I've had a rough day. Like I said, we're just having a quick drink after work."

"Well you make sure that's all it is."

Baldwin returned and Smith ordered another two drinks.

"I haven't even touched the first one yet," Baldwin said.

"Well you'd better drink up," Smith picked up the drinks and took them to his usual table on the far side of the room.

"Marge just gave me a bit of a bollocking," he said when they'd sat down.

"What for?"

"For having a drink with a colleague after work."

"What's wrong with that?"

"Marge can be a bit over-protective at times. She reckons I should be at home with Whitton and Laura."

"Maybe you should."

"Drink up. This beer is going down well. If I was sitting here with Bridge or Yang Chu, Marge wouldn't even bat an eyelid but having a drink with a pretty PC isn't right in Marge's eyes. She's a bit old fashioned like that."

"Pretty PC?"

"Marge's words, not mine. You did well back there, by the way – with James France, I mean. And you're really fitting in with the team. I'd say there's definitely a permanent place for you with us after this."

"It's better than dealing with complaints behind the front desk all day. Do you think this thing with France is going to go away?"

"More than likely. He appeared to have a change of heart back there." Smith finished what was left of his second pint.

Baldwin still had a full glass.

"I'm going to get another beer. I can't have you drinking alone."

"Can I ask you a question?" Smith sat down again. "This sounds terrible but I don't even know your first name. Ever since you arrived, you've always just been *Baldwin*."

"It's Victoria. Just please don't ever call me Vicky."

"I won't. Baldwin it is then."

She started to laugh. "Sorry, I don't usually drink beer – this stuff has gone straight to my head."

"I don't know anything about you. You've been at the station for how long?"

"Four years."

"And I don't know one thing about you other than the fact that you're a whiz behind the front desk and you're quickly becoming one hell of a detective."

"There's not much to know. I'm twenty six, I'm not married and I don't have a boyfriend. I live on my own with a cat called Frank. That's about it."

"Frank?"

"I inherited him from a neighbour."

"I'll drink to that. I inherited a dog called Fred."

"So we've got something in common then?" Baldwin's face reddened slightly.

"I think I'd better get going. Thanks for the drinks."

Smith drained his pint. "I'll give you a lift home."

"I only live around the corner. I feel like a walk. I'll see you at work tomorrow."

Smith watched as she stood up and left the pub. Marge approached and sat at the table. "I hope you know what you're doing."

"I'm not doing anything, Marge."

"I've got eyes in my head. You have a child at home remember."

"So you keep reminding me. Next time I feel like a drink after work with a colleague, I'll make sure to go somewhere where I don't have to justify myself."

Smith drove home the long way. He needed some time to think. He was feeling terrible about the way he'd spoken to Marge.

Why the hell did I have to be so rude? he thought. *Marge was only saying what I already knew. I should have gone straight home.*

He'd worked with Baldwin for four years but in recent days he'd seen her in a completely different light – she was no longer just the face behind the front desk, she'd really impressed him. And Marge was right – she was very pretty.

He put some music on and tried to think about something else. The clock on the dashboard read 19:45. He knew that Laura would probably be asleep already. He thought about his visit to Jessica Blakemore earlier in the day and wondered what dreams would lay in store for him that night. His phone started to ring. He took it out. It was Whitton.

"Hey you," he answered it. "I'm on my way home. It's been a bit of a rough day. Is everything alright?"

"Theakston and Fred had a fight," Whitton sounded quite stressed out. Her voice was shaky. "Theakston tore a bit of the Pug's ear off. It's probably worse than it looks but there was quite a bit of blood."

"What were they fighting about?" Smith knew the dogs hardly ever fought – neither of them could really be bothered.

"I don't know what caused it. They were out the back at the end of the garden and Theakston started to bark at something by the back fence. He went crazy. When Fred went to investigate, Theakston went for him."

"I'm almost home. I'm sure it's not as bad as it looks. You know how much the ear bleeds."

Smith parked the car outside the house and got out. Theakston pounced on him as soon as he got through the front door.

"He's begging for forgiveness," Whitton appeared in the doorway. "I don't know what came over him."

"Where's Fred?"

"Asleep in the living room. I bandaged his ear and he's lapping up the attention. He's lying next to Laura on the couch. Are you hungry? There's half a chicken in the oven."

"That would be great." Smith looked at the Bull Terrier by his feet. "You bad dog. Why did you attack Fred?"

"He wouldn't stop barking at something at the end of the garden. I've never heard him bark like that before. Fred was just in the wrong place at the wrong time. You said you had a bit of a rough day?"

"Me and Baldwin have been suspended."

"Suspended?"

"We've sorted it out. It'll be lifted by tomorrow."

He told her about how James France had reported them for interviewing Jonathan Collins and how he and Baldwin had persuaded him to drop the charges.

"That's why I'm a bit late," he added. "I took Baldwin to the Hog's Head for a drink afterwards."

"You took Baldwin to the Hog's Head?"

"We just had a couple of pints. To drown our sorrows."

"I see."

"What's that supposed to mean?"

"You spend all day working with the woman and then you take her out for a drink afterwards."

"What's wrong with you? This is Baldwin we're talking about."

"This is a young attractive young woman we're talking about."

"Don't tell me you're jealous?"

"Of course not – it would've been nice if you'd come straight home, that's all."

"You are jealous. Would you be carrying on like this if it'd been me and Bridge who were suspended and we'd gone out for a drink afterwards?"

"I am not jealous. I'm going to have a bath. You can fix yourself something to eat."

CHAPTER TWENTY ONE

"I don't like dogs, Bee," the big man said. "You know I don't like dogs."
"A giant like yourself is afraid of a little dog? You're pathetic."
"It wasn't a little dog. It was one of those Pit Bull things or whatever they call them. It looked straight at me. It had the devil in its eyes. I'm not going back there again."
"You'll do what I tell you to do. You owe me, remember? Or have you forgotten whose fault all of this is?"
"I'm not going back there," he'd been attacked by three German Shepherds when he was younger. His legs, arms and stomach still bore the scars.
"OK, we'll work our way around that in due course – there's still work to do before we have to tackle that one."
"I'm not going back there if that dog is there, Bee. I'm not."
"Stop calling me that. I told you I'll figure something out." She opened up a black book. It contained a list of names. She pointed to the fifth name on the list. The first three had been crossed out. "Go and run me a bath. Make it nice and hot and use some of that new bath oil I bought."

* * *

Whitton lay back in the bath, closed her eyes and sank deeper into the water. Theakston was lying on the mat next to her. Since the fight with Fred, the Bull Terrier had followed her everywhere. Whitton still couldn't understand what had brought on the fight – Theakston and Fred were usually the best of friends. Something had caused the him to flip. Whitton still didn't know what it was he'd been barking at. When she looked over the fence in the back garden there was nothing there.

She breathed in deeply and let the warm water soak her day away. She opened her eyes when Theakston started to growl.

"It's me, boy," Smith stood in the doorway. "That chicken was delicious," he said to Whitton. "Do you want me to wash your back?"

"You'll have to get past him first," Whitton nodded to her thirty kilogram bodyguard on the bathroom mat.

"I'll take my chances." Smith sat next to the bath and placed his hands on Whitton's shoulders. "Sorry about earlier."

"You don't have to say sorry. It's not you. I'm going crazy stuck at home all day."

"You're not stuck at home. You go out all the time."

"I need to get back to work. I didn't realise how much I'd miss it. I even miss Brownhill."

"You should see her now. She's lost a load of weight and it looks like she's kicked the moustache into touch for good. She almost looks like a woman."

"You're terrible. Do you think they'll let me come back early?"

"What about Laura?"

"We can put her in daycare. Or I could take her with me."

"I don't think old Smyth would allow that."

"How is the public school imbecile?"

"Still the same. He was playing Michael Bolton in his office today."

"Michael Bolton's not too bad."

"He's terrible. Not as bad as Meatloaf but almost. So you're not mad at me anymore?"

"I wasn't mad at you – I just need to get back to work."

"OK," Smith kissed her on the top of her head. "This is what we've got so far. Two women were killed. One had her face smashed in with an iron and the other was stabbed. Both of them were home alone with their young children. As far as we're aware, these women didn't know each other. The word *Unworthy* was found at both murder scenes."

"They must be connected in some way," Whitton said.

"That's what I think. But how are they connected? Julie Phelps was a bit of a wild one in her day – she'd calmed down in recent times but her colourful past was common knowledge. Magda Phillips was well off and quite reserved. She had very few friends and nobody can think of a reason why anybody would want to hurt her."

"Something has to link them together. What about the crime scenes? Webber doesn't normally miss much. What did he find?"

"Nothing that's going to help us much," Smith admitted. "A couple of size thirteen boot prints at Magda Phillips' place and nothing at Julie Phelps' house. The only thing we've got so far is a three and a half year olds' story about a huge man in the doorway."

"That would tie in with the size thirteen prints. You need to speak to the boy again."

"You've got to be joking. I got suspended for that, remember."

"But you talked the uncle into dropping the charges. Talk him into letting you interview the boy again. Do it by the book this time."

"I didn't really interview him. Baldwin did most of the talking. He drew this picture and when I asked him what all the black in the doorway was, he told me the man was too big for the door."

"Maybe he can draw the man in more detail," Whitton suggested. "What have you got to lose? This water's getting cold."

Smith helped her out and handed her a towel. "I'm just going to check on Laura. Do you want a beer?"

"Sounds great."

Smith went downstairs. He heard the sound of the Pug's snoring before he even reached the living room. Fred was lying on his back on the couch. He was fast asleep. Laura was lying next to him. Smith smiled and went through to the kitchen. He took two beers out the fridge and took one of them outside to the garden. He lit a cigarette and walked to the fence at the back. Behind the fence was an alleyway where the wheelie bins were stored. Smith took a long drag on the cigarette and exhaled a huge cloud of smoke. He could see where Theakston had gone crazy. The grass was ripped up in places and there were spatters of mud on the six foot fence. Spots of blood were mixed in with the mud.

"He was barking there for ages," Whitton appeared behind him. She was holding a beer in her hand. "I couldn't stop him."

"It was probably a cat," Smith suggested. "Theakston has never liked cats." He looked over the fence. It was starting to get dark and there wasn't much to see. His wheelie bin was still in the same place as were those of his neighbours.

Probably a cat

It was too dark for Smith to see the size thirteen boot print in the dirt behind the fence.

CHAPTER TWENTY TWO

The dreams Smith were dreading didn't happen. He was woken by the sound of Theakston barking in the back garden. He went to the curtain and looked outside. The dog was by the fence again – he was trying to jump over the six foot barrier but he was too fat. Fred was watching him. He was giving the Bull Terrier a wide berth. After their altercation the day before, the repulsive Pug wasn't going to risk a repeat performance. Smith went downstairs, made some coffee and took it outside to the garden. Whitton was sitting on the bench. Laura lay on a blanket on the grass.

"What time is it?" Smith asked.

"Just after seven," Whitton replied. "I thought I'd let you sleep for a while. You seemed so peaceful lying there." She pointed to the baby. "That little lady slept the whole night through – there must be something in the air."

"What's got into that dog?" Smith looked at Theakston. He was still jumping up at the fence.

"You were probably right about that cat. He can no doubt still smell it. What time do you have to be in this morning?"

"Brownhill wanted us in about ten minutes ago but seeing as though I've been suspended I can use that as an excuse. I doubt Smyth's even up yet. You know what he's like – he'll probably swan in around ten so I've got a few hours to spend with my two favourite ladies. How about taking Laura and the dogs down to the park for an hour or so?"

"Sounds good. Do you think the suspension will be lifted?"

"Of course. Once James France drops the ridiculous charges Smyth will have no option but to reinstate us."

The sound of Smith's mobile phone ringing inside could be heard. Smith knew instinctively that his morning off with his family was about to be cancelled.

He went back inside to answer it. It was DI Brownhill.

"Morning, boss," Smith said. "What can I do for you?"

"There's been another one. A young woman was found in Newbeck Park this morning."

"That's just down the road from my house." It was the same park he was planning on taking his family to.

"I know. A jogger found her about an hour ago. It looks like she's been strangled."

"Do you think it's our *Unworthy* killer?"

"We don't know yet. Grant and I are on our way there now. As is DC Yang Chu. Bridge isn't answering his phone. I want you there as soon as possible."

"I'm suspended, remember?"

"Not anymore. James France has had the charges dropped."

"Give me ten minutes then."

* * *

Smith made it in five. Two police cars and an ambulance were already at the scene. Brownhill and Webber still hadn't arrived. Smith got out the car and walked the familiar route towards the lake. He'd lost count of how many times he'd walked this path – first with Theakston and more recently with his daughter. The park was a place he always came to forget about everything and now a woman had been killed here. Two PC's were standing in front of a police tape by the path. A middle aged man was sitting on the bench where Smith had sat many times waiting for Theakston to wear himself out. The man's face was very pale. Smith walked over to the two PCs. The dead woman was lying on her back on a verge of grass next to the path. Her face was blue and bloated and her eyes bulged open. Her neck was heavily bruised. Smith could tell straight away that she'd been dead for quite some time.

Yang Chu approached. "I came as soon as I could." He looked at the woman lying on the grass. "Do we know who she is?"

"Not yet," Smith said. "Apparently a jogger found her about an hour ago."

"That'll be him, sir," one of the PCs pointed to the man on the bench.

Smith bent down to get a closer look at the woman. She had bleached blonde hair – it had turned black at the roots, and she was very slightly built. She was wearing a black skirt, a white blouse and a pair of high-heeled shoes.

She wasn't out for an early morning stroll dressed like that, Smith thought.

"Do you think it's our *Unworthy* guy?" Yang Chu asked.

"There's nothing to suggest that it is yet," Smith said. "I don't want to move her until Webber has finished but I can't see anything that would point to the same killer as the other two."

Brownhill and Webber walked towards them down the path. They were walking so close together that Smith was sure they were holding hands.

"And they say romance is dead," he whispered to Yang Chu. "An early morning soiree to a murder scene."

"You're terrible, Sarge," Yang Chu said but he couldn't hide the smile on his face.

"Keep those people away please," Webber told the two PC's. A crowd of people had now gathered in the park.

"Morning, Webber," Smith said. He nodded to Brownhill. "Morning boss. Lovely day for it."

"Where's the man who found her?" the DI asked.

"Over on that bench. He doesn't look too healthy for a jogger."

"Go and speak to him. Let Grant do his job."

"One thing, boss. I don't think she was killed where the jogger found her."

"What makes you say that?"

"Go and have a look. She's been dead for a while. I'd say at least 24 hours. She would've been found earlier than this morning if she was killed here. It's been very warm for this time of year – the park's been busy."

"Thank you for your insight. Go and speak to that pasty faced jogger."

The jogger had regained some of the colour in his face when Smith sat down next to him. He smelled heavily of sweat.

"I'm DS Smith. Can I have a word?"

The man shuffled uneasily on the bench. "Dan Green. The wife thought I needed to lose a few pounds so I started jogging. I still can't believe there's a dead woman over there." He pointed to the police tape.

"What time did you find the woman?"

"Around six. The park's quiet then – I like to have it to myself."

"Do you know who the woman is?"

"Never seen her before. Did you see her face?"

"Which route do you take around the park?"

"I start off at the entrance by the lake and make my way up. I was about to have a rest when I spotted her. Who would possibly do such a thing?"

"We'll find out. Did you see anybody else around early this morning?"

"Not a soul." He looked at his watch. "I have to get to work. I don't know what else I can tell you."

"OK," Smith agreed. "We'll need you to come to the station to make a statement but that can be arranged at your convenience."

Dan stood up. "I don't think I'm going to forget that face for a very long time."

Smith walked back to where the body had been found. Grant Webber was talking on his phone. He appeared to be very angry. DI Brownhill was keeping her distance from the head of forensics.

"What's up with Webber?" Smith asked her.

"He's trying to get hold of his team," Brownhill told him. "They're taking their time about it."

"Did he find any ID on the woman?"

"Nothing. She had no handbag, purse or any other personal belongings. If I didn't agree with your theory that she wasn't killed here, I'd put it down to a straightforward robbery gone wrong. Mugger tries to steal her handbag – she puts up a fight and gets killed in the process."

"But she wasn't killed here was she?"

"We'll know more when Grant's team gets their arses into gear but, no, I don't think she was. I've seen bodies before and I'd say this one's been dead for at least two days. The tissue on her face and hands is starting to show signs of rigor."

"She was killed somewhere else and dumped here. Why?"

"That's what we need to find out. But first we need to ascertain who she is."

"Somebody must be missing her. She was dressed quite smartly – white blouse, black skirt and high heels, the sort of clothes a woman might wear on a night out."

Webber finished up on the phone and came over. "They're on their way."

"What do you think?" Smith asked him.

"I don't think this is where she was killed. If I were to hazard a guess I'd say she's been dead for over 24 hours. And if that's the case I reckon she was dumped here sometime last night."

"Thanks, Webber," Smith said. "I thought so. This park is busy during the day – I know, I come here quite often, so someone would definitely have seen her if she was here yesterday. Did you find anything else?"

"The bruises on her neck. The path guys will have to confirm it of course but the pattern of the bruises suggest whoever strangled her had big hands."

"Did you look for any boot prints?"

"Size thirteen, you mean?"

"I just want to know for sure if this is another victim of our *Unworthy* killer."
"Nothing. And there's no sign of any writing anywhere near her. I think you might be looking at a different murderer altogether."

Two of Webber's team arrived and Smith decided to get out of there. He walked towards the small lake. He knew the paths around the park off by heart. He'd been coming here for years. He kept the lake to his right and continued to where the path ran through a small patch of trees. The path came out at one of only two entrance gates.

The killer came along here. He carried her all this way.

Smith estimated the distance from the entrance by the road to where the woman was found to be roughly four hundred metres. The woman wasn't overweight but she wasn't light either.

It was the same man who killed Julie Phelps and Magda Phillips.

Smith didn't know why but he was sure this was the work of the same killer. He walked through the gate and emerged onto the road. The road was busy – the early morning rush hour traffic was in full force. He realised that in the early hours of the morning there would be nobody around. It would be easy to park a car by the entrance and carry a body into the park without being seen.

He walked back to where the body had been found. More people had gathered to see what had happened. A PC was fighting a losing battle trying to get them to disperse.

"There's nothing to see here," the desperation was obvious in his voice. "Please clear the area and let us do our jobs."

"Move it, you lot," Smith said so loudly, he surprised himself. "This is none of your business."

It seemed to do the trick. The crowd of people slowly thinned out until only Grant Webber and two of his team were left.

"Thanks," the head of forensics looked at Smith. "I didn't know you could be so forceful."

"I've been learning a few tricks from Brownhill."

Webber carefully lifted the dead woman's head. The bluish-grey bruises spread all the way round her neck.

"It looks like she died from the strangulation. There are no other obvious injuries. We'll know more when the path guys are finished with her but I'd say that's how she died."

A woman in her mid twenties approached from the lake-side of the path. She was walking a young German Shepherd. The dog tugged at its lead when they got closer to where the dead woman lay.

"Jack," the woman said. "Get back here." She tugged at the lead but the young dog was too strong. "Jack!" she tugged the lead harder.

She glanced at the object of the dog's curiosity and gasped. Her eyes rested on the dead woman in the bushes. Then she looked at Smith.

"That's Joy. She's my boss. That's Joy Williams."

CHAPTER TWENTY THREE

"Joy Williams," Smith said in DI Brownhill's office.
Yang Chu and Baldwin sat on either side of him. Baldwin wasn't wearing her uniform for once – she had on a pair of black jeans and a green blouse. Bridge was missing in action once again.
"Thirty two years old," Smith continued. "She worked in IT at some big-shot company in the city centre. According to her PA she was last seen at Golding's – it's a fancy restaurant on the river. They were out celebrating a new contract on Tuesday night."
"What time was this?" Brownhill asked.
"She left the restaurant at around half ten. Said she had to get back for the babysitter – she has an eighteen month old daughter."
"How did she get home?" Baldwin asked.
"She said she was going to get a taxi."
"I'll check," Yang Chu offered and left the office.
"What about a husband? Boyfriend? The father of the baby?"
"Apparently, he did a runner shortly after the baby was born."
"Where the hell is Bridge?" Brownhill said. "His attitude these days stinks. He's not doing himself any favours for the DS position."
"He'll be here," Smith insisted. "Joy Williams' body is in the hands of the path guys so we'll know more when they're done with her but Webber and me both reckon she died from strangulation. And she wasn't killed in the park."

Yang Chu came back in. "She got in a City Taxi at ten thirty five on Tuesday night. "She went straight home."
"We'll need her address," Smith said.
"48 Turnbill Road."

"Let's get straight there, then. Boss," he turned to Brownhill. "Can you let your man, Webber know where we are? The other two women were killed at home. My gut is telling me this one's no different."

"So you're inclined to believe this is another *Unworthy* killing?" Brownhill asked.

"I am. Come on, Baldwin. Let's go and take a look."

* * *

Smith and Baldwin got out of the car outside number 48 Turnbill Road. The house was a neat semi-detached place with a small garden at the front. The first thing Smith noticed was that the curtains were drawn in all the windows.

"This doesn't look good," he said. "This doesn't look good at all."

He walked up the path and knocked on the door. No answer. The faint sound of crying could be heard from inside. Smith turned the handle. The door was open. The crying got louder as he and Baldwin stepped inside. Smith went through to the living room and opened the curtains.

"Triple glazing," he pointed to the glass. "She'd had the place nicely soundproofed."

The crying appeared to get louder. Another sound could be heard mixed in with it – a low moaning noise.

"Stay here," Smith told Baldwin and went upstairs.

He found the source of the crying. A baby girl was standing up in a cot in the back bedroom. Her eyes were puffy and red and her lips were dry. She had dried vomit on her chest.

"It's alright, baby," Smith picked her out of the cot. "You're going to be alright. Baldwin," he shouted down the stairs. "Could you help me up here? I think this little lady could do with something to drink. I want to have a look around."

Baldwin took the baby downstairs and Smith checked the rest of the bedrooms. The main bedroom was empty. The bed was made and the curtains drawn. The spare bedroom was also empty. The bathroom door was closed. The low moaning sound could be heard again from inside. Smith opened the door and went in. A young woman was lying on the floor next to the bath. Her hands and feet were bound and her mouth was gagged. A thick chain had been wrapped around her waist and attached to the base of the sink pedestal. Above the sink was a mirror. The word *Unworthy* was written on the glass in what appeared to be black marker pen.

Smith bent down.

"It's going to be alright." He removed the cloth from her mouth. "Don't try to speak. I'll get you something to drink."

He left the bathroom, returned with a beaker and filled it half full of water from the bathroom tap. "Sip it slowly. You're dehydrated – too much and you'll be sick. An ambulance is on the way."

"Rose," the woman said through cracked lips. "Is Rose OK?"

"She'll be fine. We got here in time. Save your strength. You need to be checked over."

Smith heard the front door open and went downstairs. Grant Webber was standing in the hallway with one of his forensics officers.

"What have we got?" he asked Smith.

"There's a young woman in the bathroom upstairs. She's pretty dehydrated but it looks like she'll be fine. There's an ambulance on the way. Baldwin is looking after the baby."

He told Webber about the writing on the bathroom mirror.

"Same killer then?" Webber sighed.

"The young woman has been chained to the sink and her hands and legs have been tied with heavy duty cable ties. We'll need something to cut them off."

"I've got some bolt cutters in the car. I want to check for prints first."
"Make it quick. That woman needs medical attention and we need to speak to her as soon as possible. She may have seen who killed Joy Williams.

Smith went outside and lit a cigarette. An ambulance pulled up to the kerb. Behind it was Yang Chu's Ford Focus. Yang Chu got out with Bridge in tow.

"I had to drag him out of bed," Yang Chu pointed to a very pale-looking DC Bridge. "Looks like he had a rough night."

"The DI is gunning for you," Smith told Bridge. "You'd better get your act together. She can put a spanner in the works for the DS position, you know."

"I had an offer I couldn't refuse," Bridge grinned.

"Well next time refuse it. We've got our hands full at the moment and I need you all to have clear heads."

"What's the story with the ambulance?" Yang Chu asked.

"There's an 18 month old baby girl in there," Smith replied. "And the babysitter. They're both dehydrated but it looks like they'll be fine. The babysitter was chained to the sink upstairs. I think she may have seen our killer."

"Then we need to speak to her," Bridge said.

"All in good time. She needs to go to the hospital to be checked over. In the meantime, I suggest you go home and have a cold shower. When will you ever grow up?"

"When there are no more women in the world. You've got boring since the baby arrived."

"Go home. Shower and change your clothes. Swill some mouthwash round, too. You still stink of booze."

Two paramedics appeared in the doorway with the babysitter on a stretcher. Baldwin emerged behind them with Joy Williams' daughter.

"I'll go with them in the ambulance," she said.

"We'll meet you at the hospital," Smith said. "We need to speak to that babysitter."

"Her name's Katie Laing. She doesn't appear to be too badly hurt. She has a few scrapes on her arms and legs from the cable ties but, apart from slight dehydration, she should be fine."

Smith threw his cigarette on the ground and stubbed it out with his foot. "Me and Yang Chu will follow in my car. Bridge, you take Yang Chu's Focus, go home and freshen up a bit. I'm calling a case briefing for twelve noon. Make sure you're there."

"Not a chance in hell," Yang Chu protested. "He's not driving my car. Why can't he use your old banger?"

"OK," Smith was in no mood to argue. He handed Bridge his car keys. "Get there as soon as you can."

CHAPTER TWENTY FOUR

"The girl's still alive. They took her away in an ambulance. I saw it myself. How could you have been so stupid? She saw your face."

"They won't find her, Bee. I chained her to the sink. They won't find her."

"Are you deaf or just plain stupid? I watched them take her away in the ambulance. She looked fine to me. That DS Smith is probably getting a beautiful description out of her as we speak. How could you have been so stupid? Why didn't you wait for her to leave first? You should have killed the babysitter."

"You didn't tell me to kill her."

"When are you going to start using your brain? Do I have to do everything for you?"

"But, Bee..."

"And stop calling me that. I need to think. And you need to stay indoors for a few days. You can't go outside." She slapped him so hard across the face that she knocked him sideways. *"I need to think – you might have ruined everything."*

* * *

Katie Laing was sitting up in the hospital bed when Smith and Yang Chu came in. A saline drip was attached to her arm. She looked a lot better than she'd done in the bathroom at Joy Williams' house.

"How are you feeling?" Smith pulled up a chair and sat next to the bed.

"I still can't believe it," Katie replied. "It doesn't seem real. He must have been in the house the whole time. He was huge."

"Are you up to telling us what happened?"

"I think so. Where's Rose?"

"She's in the nursery here. She's going to be fine."

"He must have been in the house the whole time," Katie said again. "I thought I'd locked the front door but I must have forgotten."

"Can you go through it all with us? Take your time. I know how hard this must be."

"I went to check on Rose. She was sleeping like a log. She's a really good sleeper."

"What time was this?" Yang Chu asked.

"Just before nine. The news hadn't started yet. I went to use the bathroom and he grabbed me from behind. He was so strong. He stuffed something in my mouth and tied me up. I was terrified. I thought he was going to kill me."

"Then what happened?" Smith said.

"Nothing. That was the scariest part – the waiting, not knowing what he was going to do to me. Rose was asleep the whole time. At least that's one thing."

"Go on," Smith urged.

"I lay there in the bathroom for what seemed like days. All these thoughts were running through my head. What was he was going to do? Why had he just left me there? What if he wanted to hurt the baby? Then, I heard the sound of the front door. I knew it had to be Joy. I tried to scream out – to warn her but my mouth was gagged. I heard her come up the stairs and go into Rose's room."

She stopped there and started to shake.

"It's alright," Smith said.

"Joy came in the bathroom and saw me tied up on the floor. She tried to help me but he came up behind her. I tried to warn her but I couldn't. I should have warned her."

"It's not your fault," Yang Chu assured her.

"He grabbed her and strangled her right in front of me. She tried to fight him off but he was too strong. He was huge."

A nurse came in, checked the drip attached to Katie's arm and left again.
"What did this man do after he'd strangled Mrs Williams?" Smith asked her.
"He dragged her out of the room. He must have dragged her down the stairs because I heard the front door open and close and I'm sure I heard the sound of a car door. I could be wrong."
"Then what happened?" Yang Chu asked.
"I tried to untie the cable ties but they were too tight. Then…" she started to cry. "I'm sorry. I still can't believe this has happened."
"It's alright," Smith said. "We're almost done. Go on."
"I heard the front door open and close again and he came back to the bathroom. I thought that it was all over for me - I was going to die – he was carrying a long, thick piece of chain. He put it around my waist and locked it around the bottom of the sink. Then the strangest thing happened. I closed my eyes and prayed. I don't even believe in God but I prayed for my life. I half expected a blow to the head but it didn't come. When I opened my eyes again, he was still standing there. He was looking at the mirror. Then he took out a pen and wrote something on it."

Unworthy, Smith thought.

"Did you know this man?" he asked.
"No, but he was definitely somebody I'd recognise if I saw him again. He was huge – at least six foot six and big with it."
"Did you get a good look at his face?" Yang Chu asked.
"That's the scariest thing. He had a very friendly face. Droopy eyes and a jolly mouth."
"I need to ask you to work with our photo-fit guy when you're feeling up to it. It would be better to do that sooner rather than later – while the memory of the events are still fresh in your head."

"I'm ready. Do you think you'll catch this man?"

"We will," Smith said even though he wasn't convinced.

None of it made any sense. Three women had been killed with their children nearby. The first two were killed at home and left there. Why did this man dump Joy Williams' body in the park afterwards? Surely it would have been less risky to leave her where he'd strangled her. And why did he leave the babysitter unharmed? She'd seen his face – it was all very baffling. These were all questions he'd have to address at the investigation briefing later that day.

"OK, Miss Laing," he said. "Thank you for your time – you've been a great help. I'll arrange for the photo-fit guy to come in later this morning. And if you think of anything else, please give me a ring on this number." He placed a card on the table next to her.

CHAPTER TWENTY FIVE

"Right," Smith said in the small conference room. "Listen up."
Brownhill, Yang Chu, Baldwin and Bridge were all seated. Bridge looked much healthier than he'd done earlier that morning. He'd had a shower and put on a clean set of clothes.

"The path report has come in," Smith continued. "Joy Williams died around half ten on Tuesday night. Cause of death was strangulation. We've spoken to the babysitter, Katie Laing and she witnessed the whole thing so we knew that already. Webber didn't find any prints at the scene but we have something better – a good description of the man who did this. White male, roughly six foot six and big with it. Friendly face and droopy eyes. Miss Laing described him as being incredibly strong."

"Somebody like that shouldn't be too hard to find," Bridge had definitely woken up. "Put his description all over the press. Somebody must know who he is."

"Hold your horses. I'd thought of that. It could have an adverse affect – it might just scare him away and make him disappear for good. I've decided to take a risk and wait a day or two before we release his description to the general public."

"Are you sure?" Brownhill said. "Why not put his face all over the place and flush him out?"

"Because this whole thing has me baffled," Smith admitted. "The first two women were killed at home and left there. Why did he dump Joy Williams' body in the park?"

"And why kill her in front of the babysitter?" Baldwin added.

"Exactly. He was taking a huge risk on both counts. The babysitter saw his face. We know he's a cold-blooded killer – why not kill the babysitter to shut her up?"

The door opened and DCI Bob Chalmers came in.

"Afternoon," Chalmers said. "Mind if I sit in? I've forgotten what it feels like to be a detective. Smyth is at a conference in Brussels for a few days and I thought I'd take advantage of his absence."

"Good to have you here, boss," Smith said.

He filled the DCI in on what they had so far. Chalmers listened intently.

"Hmm," he said when Smith had finished. "Well I'll be damned if this isn't the most bizarre investigation I've ever come across. What are your thoughts so far?"

"That's the problem," Smith said. "We're not sure. We're positive it's the same killer – the word *Unworthy* links the murders together, but we're still no closer to finding out why? Why is this man doing this?"

"Is there anything that links these three women together?"

"Not as far as we know. Julie Phelps was killed while her husband was away. She had a rather shady past but she seemed to have cleaned up her act since her baby was born. Megan Collins was a widow with a few bob in the bank and Joy Williams worked for an IT firm that seems to be going places. Her husband left shortly after the baby came along."

Chalmers' phone started to ring in his pocket. He took it out, looked at the screen and frowned.

"Smyth. No rest for the wicked. There has to be a connection between these three women. Concentrate on that connection before you do anything else."

He nodded to Smith and left the room.

"I'm inclined to agree with the DCI," Brownhill said.

"Me too," Smith agreed.

"I still say we plaster this bloke's face all over the papers," Bridge chipped in. "We'll catch the bastard a lot quicker if we do that."

"No," Smith said. "We find out what links these women together. This guy isn't just selecting his victims at random – he's working to a careful plan."

"Maybe he's finished," Yang Chu suggested. "Maybe that's why he let the babysitter see his face. He could've left the country already for all we know."

"I'm not so sure about that," Smith said.

"How do you reckon that one?"

"Something in my gut tells me he's far from finished."

"That famous Smith gut instinct again?" Brownhill said. Her tone was serious. "Right, this is how we're going to play it – Smith, you and Baldwin seem to be working well together so I'd like to keep that momentum going. Look deep into the pasts of these three women. See if their paths have crossed at any point. Bridge, I want you and Yang Chu to speak to Joy Williams' neighbours. I want the whole street covered – somebody might have seen a strange car parked outside on Tuesday night. This man carried the body out of the house. He must have had a vehicle nearby."

"There's something else I thought about," Baldwin said.

"Go on."

"Joy Williams was killed on Tuesday night. Her body wasn't found in the park until this morning. If the killer dumped her in the park straight after he killed her, someone would have found her yesterday. The park is busy at this time of the year. Where was the body kept until then and why wait?"

"It's a valid point," Brownhill said. "But I don't think it's our main priority at the moment. We'll go through that at a later stage. Let's get to it then."

* * *

"Where are we going, Sarge?" Baldwin asked Smith as they drove away from the car park at the station.

"There's somebody I'd like you to meet. I think you two will get on well."

"You're going to see Jessica Blakemore aren't you? The crazy shrink."

"She's not crazy – she's just a bit misunderstood. You'll see."

"I have met her before, you know. I bumped into her a few times during the Selene Lupei investigation a couple of years ago."

"I just want to ask her a few questions."

"Brownhill won't be too impressed."

"Brownhill will never know."

They drove in silence out of the city towards the Lemonwood Hospital. Smith parked as close to the entrance as possible and got out the car.

"Let me speak to her first," he told Baldwin outside the main door. "Jessica is a bit world-weary. She tends to have an inbuilt mechanism that makes her automatically distrust people."

"It's probably for the best these days."

"I'm getting to like you more and more each day."

Smith walked up to the reception desk. The same woman who'd been there a few days earlier was busy on the telephone. She smiled at Smith and cupped her hand over the mouthpiece. "You can go through."

Smith was gobsmacked.

The receptionist ended her call. "I don't know what you did but Miss Blakemore seemed to brighten up quite a bit after your last visit. Dr Grace has given me the authority to let you see her whenever you need to."

"Thank you," Smith walked down the corridor shaking his head.

Baldwin followed behind him.

Jessica Blakemore was sitting in the day room. She was writing something in a black notebook. Two men were engaged in a game of chess on the other side of the room. Both of them were studying the board intently. Jessica looked up when she heard Smith and Baldwin come in.

"Back so soon? People are going to start talking. Shall we go outside? The walls have ears and those two so-called chess players haven't moved a piece in over three days. They're spies."

Baldwin's eyes widened.

"I'm winding you up, PC Baldwin. I'm nuts, remember. Let's go. He can't go five minutes without a cigarette and we're not allowed to smoke inside anymore."

"What do you need to know?" Jessica chose a bench in the shade. "Take a seat."

Smith and Baldwin sat down opposite her.

"Our *Unworthy* killer has struck again," Smith began. "And this time we have a witness – a young woman saw the whole thing and she's given us a good description."

"So why are you here? What do you need me for? Put the description out and arrest the miscreant."

"I just wanted to ask you something first."

"Did the murdered woman have a child?"

"An eighteen month old girl."

"And the word *Unworthy* was written somewhere nearby?"

"On the mirror in the bathroom where she was killed. Her body was found a day and a half later in the park down the road from my house. The park is nowhere near where the dead woman lived. We don't know why the killer changed the pattern and took the body away from the scene of the crime."

"You said there was a witness?"

"The woman's babysitter saw everything – she saw the killer's face and yet he didn't kill her."

"She wasn't unworthy."

"Excuse me?"

"The babysitter. She wasn't the one the murderer came there to kill."

Smith took out his cigarettes and lit one. "This makes no sense at all."

Jessica gave him a look she'd given him once before. It was the expression she used when Smith stated the obvious. "Since when has murder ever made sense? You said the killer was a man?"

"Did I?"

"You said '*he* didn't kill her'. That's the part that doesn't make any sense to me."

"And his description matches the one we got from a young boy who may have seen his mother's killer," Baldwin joined in.

Jessica looked Baldwin up and down. "Does it now? Then this is very odd. Was there any sign of sexual abuse on any of the victims?"

"None at all," Baldwin replied. "It appears his sole purpose was to kill these women."

"In the majority of documented cases where a man has killed more than two women, there is a sexual element involved. More often than not, the killing is merely a necessity to cover his tracks after he's achieved gratification. It is extremely rare for the motive to be anything else apart from sexual. Unless…"

"Unless what?" Smith said.

"Let me mull it over for the rest of the afternoon. I assume the lovely Bryony Brownhill doesn't know about this visit?"

"What do you think?"

"And now you have a partner in crime," she smiled at Baldwin. "Give me a few hours to process all this. I have a theory but I need to put a few things in order first. I'll phone you when I'm finished. This is all very close to home isn't it, detective? What with the baby and everything. How's the dreaming coming along?"

"Under control," Smith lied. "I'll be waiting for you call."

CHAPTER TWENTY SIX

TWENTY YEARS EARLIER

"Look what you've done."
Bee had been in surgery for three hours. Her mother and younger brother sat by her bedside in the hospital.
"Look what you've done now."
Her brother couldn't even bring himself to look at his sister. He could still hear the resounding crack of the branch in his ears as it broke free from the tree and fell on top of her.
"I didn't mean it," he said.
"You never do."

"Mrs Hall," a man in white came in. "Can I speak to you?"
Bee's brother watched as his mother left the room with the doctor.
"I didn't mean it, Bee," he said to his sleeping sister. "It just broke. I didn't know it was going to break."

"She's going to be alright," Dr Cannon said. "She ought to make a full recovery. The operation was successful. There is something you need to know, however. She's suffered a gynecologic hemorrhage – the impact of the heavy branch resulted in severe internal bleeding and I'm afraid we had to perform an emergency hysterectomy."
"I don't understand."
"The trauma to her abdomen meant we had no other option. We had to remove most of the uterus. I'm afraid she'll never be able to have children."

CHAPTER TWENTY SEVEN

"I like her," Baldwin said as they drove away from the hospital. "I don't think there's anything wrong with her."
"She's no more crazy than most of the people out here," Smith mused. "And she's given me plenty of advice in the past."
"What do you think she meant about the motive for these murders?"
"Only time will tell."
Smith turned left onto the main road into the city. A huge billboard on the side of the road was trying to tell him that Autumn was still quite a way off – it depicted a scene of 'family bliss' with a father pushing sausages around on a small barbeque. He suddenly came up with an idea.
"What are you doing this Saturday?" he asked Baldwin.
"Same as usual," Baldwin replied. "Not much."
"It's Erica's birthday and I'm going to make a big deal out of it. The summer seems to be determined to hang around for a bit – I'm going to invite everyone round for a good old fashioned Aussie Barbie at our place."
"Sounds great."
"It'll be good for Erica. She can catch up with everyone. She's really missing work. I think I'll even invite Brownhill and Webber."

Smith's phone started to ring. He took it out and handed it to Baldwin.
"It's the DI," she said.
"See what she wants."
"Ma'am," Baldwin answered it. "Smith's driving."
"Where are you?" Brownhill asked.
Baldwin had to think fast. She didn't want to tell the DI that they'd been to see Jessica Blakemore. "We're on our way to see the owner of the IT company where Joy Williams worked."
Smith turned and gave her the thumbs up.

"I want you back here at three for an emergency briefing. Tell Smith I want to speak to him when he's not driving."

"Will do, Ma'am." Baldwin rang off.

"The DI wants you to call her when you get the chance," she said to Smith. "She mentioned something about an emergency briefing at three."

"Journalists," Smith stopped at a red traffic light. "It was only a matter of time before that lot got wind of this. If she thinks I'm heading up another press conference, she's got another thing coming. I hate those vultures. Do we know the address of that IT company?"

"Hold on," Baldwin took out her phone.

She found it straight away. Love IT dominated the first page of the Google search. Baldwin had to admit the name was very catchy.

"They have an office on Gillygate," she said. "Number 16. It's just round the corner from the Minster."

"I know Gillygate," Smith performed an illegal U-Turn and headed towards the city centre.

The offices of Love IT were closed when they got there. A sign on the door told them they would be open again on Monday. There was an emergency number on the sign.

Smith took out his phone and dialled it. It went straight to voicemail. A man's voice informed him that the offices of Love IT would be open again on Monday. In the event of an IT emergency, could he leave a message after the tone. Smith remembered something about a lucrative new contract Love IT had just signed.

"Good Day," he said. "I'm phoning regarding the contract signed on Tuesday. There seem to be a few irregularities pertaining to Love IT that we need to clarify before going forward. I'm out of the office at the moment but if you could phone me on this number, I'd very much like to speak to you with regards to our future business dealings."

Smith's phone rang almost straight away.

"You're terrible," Baldwin was beaming from ear to ear.

"Smith," Smith answered the call.

"Who is this?" a man's voice asked.

"Who is this?"

"Kenneth Love. Of Love IT. What's this about irregularities with the new contract?"

"That wasn't exactly the truth. My name is detective sergeant Jason Smith. Is there somewhere we can speak? It's very important."

The line went quiet for a moment. "What's this all about, detective?"

"I'd rather not talk over the phone."

"I'm at home right now." He gave Smith the address.

* * *

Ten minutes later, Smith parked the car outside the address Kenneth Love had given him. It was a brand new apartment building overlooking the river. The parking spaces were all allocated to the residents. Smith parked in the spot reserved for a Mrs Hannah Dunn and got out the car.

Baldwin gazed up at the impressive modern structure. "This place must have cost a few bob. Where does all this money come from?"

"I hate money," Smith mused. "Let's go and speak with this Mr Love before the lady whose parking spot I've nicked comes back."

Kenneth Love's apartment was on the second floor. Smith contemplated the lift but decided against it. "Let's take the stairs. I don't trust those things."

They found number 4 and Smith rang the bell. Kenneth Love opened the door with a troubled expression on his face.

"What's going on? Has something happened to Abi?"

"Can we come in?" Smith asked.

"Of course," Love stepped to the side. "Come through to the living room."

He led them down a corridor to a huge room. Large glass windows covered the whole of one side of the room. Baldwin looked down at the river below. Tourists were still enjoying boat cruises up and down the river.

"What's going on?" Love asked again.

Smith sat down on a two seater leather couch. "It's about one of your employees, Mr Love. Joy Williams. I'm afraid she was found in the Newbeck Park this morning. She's dead."

"Dead?"

"She'd been strangled," Baldwin was still staring at the boats on the river.

"Murdered?" Love said in a voice no more than a whisper.

"We know she was killed some time on Tuesday night," Smith told him. "We have a witness who saw the whole thing."

"Good Lord," Love said. "Who would want to kill Joy?" Something seemed to change in his whole demeanour. He started to frown. "What has this got to do with me?"

"We're led to believe you saw Joy on Tuesday night," Baldwin said.

"You were one of the last people to see her alive," Smith added. "How was she on Tuesday night?"

"What do you mean?"

"Was there anything bothering her?" Smith elaborated.

"No, of course not. We were out celebrating – we'd just signed the biggest contract since the company started. We were all set to become very well off – Joy included. Why would there be anything bothering her?"

Smith decided on a change of tack. "How long have you known Mrs Williams?"

"She's been with us from the beginning. I started the company three years ago."

"And what is it you do?" Baldwin moved away from the window and sat down next to Smith.

"IT. We started off by offering IT solutions for small businesses but we'd moved forward in the past few months. The contract we signed on Tuesday means we'll be overseeing the security in some of the big department stores around the country."

"Sounds impressive," Smith said. "Joy had an eighteen month old girl. Didn't that pose a problem for her with work?"

"Not at all. A lot of the work we do can be undertaken from anywhere in the country. IT is boundless. I still can't believe someone would want to kill Joy."

"How did you meet Joy?" Smith asked.

"She was recommended by an old colleague. He'd known Joy for years. They did the same computer course at college, I think."

"So you've only known Joy since she started to work at Love IT?" Baldwin asked.

"That's right."

"We'll need the name of that old colleague," Smith said.

Love sat with his head in his hands. It appeared that the reality of the news Smith and Baldwin had brought to him was really starting to sink in. "That poor child. What's going to happen to the child? The father is a complete waste of space. Ran off as soon as the baby was born."

"We'd better get going," Smith said. "Thank you for your time. We need the name of the man who recommended Joy for the job."

Love stood up and walked over to a huge oak desk. He took out a notepad and wrote a name and number on it. "It makes all of this seem rather insignificant, doesn't it?" He gazed out of the window down to the river below. "Money, I mean. When something like this happens, it makes you want to question what's really important."

CHAPTER TWENTY EIGHT

"You've been clamped, Sarge." Baldwin pointed out when they stood outside Kenneth Love's apartment block.
The bright yellow wheel clamp contrasted dramatically with the red of Smith's Ford Sierra. Smith looked around for the culprit but there was nobody there.
"Bastards," he said. "This is what's wrong with this country at the moment. We can't even do our jobs without some jobsworth making life difficult for us."
"They probably didn't know it was a detective sergeant's car."
"I don't care. How long were we in there?" he pointed up to the apartment. "Fifteen minutes, tops? This is bullshit."

He spotted the reason for the offensive yellow wheel clamp fifty metres away. A short man in a green tracksuit was watching them closely. Smith approached him. "Could you get that monstrosity off my car right now?"
"You're parked in Mrs Dunn's spot," the man said. "Rules are rules."
"And who might you be? That tracksuit doesn't look like a traffic warden's uniform."
"This is private land. The body corporate own the building and the parking area – it doesn't come under the jurisdiction of the city council. I'm the caretaker here."
Baldwin stepped in. "Sir, I assume you're aware of the new legislation. Clamping on private property is actually against the law."
Smith took out his ID. "Which means you've clamped the wrong car, arsehole."
The little caretaker looked like he was about to cry. "I don't make the rules. The body corporate are a rule unto themselves."
"You've got two minutes," Smith told him.

Smith drove off three minutes later leaving a very dejected looking caretaker behind him. He clutched the wheel clamp to his chest like it was a teddy bear.

"Is clamping on private land really against the law?" Smith asked Baldwin.

"It is. They passed a law a couple of years ago. Why, did you actually think I'd made it up?"

"It did cross my mind." He turned right and drove across the bridge towards the city centre. "I'm starving. I haven't eaten since last night."

"We've got half an hour before the briefing, Sarge. And shouldn't you phone Brownhill? The DI wanted to speak to you, remember?"

"It can wait. My stomach is growling at me."

He parked on double yellow lines next to a bakery and left the engine running. "Stay here," he said to Baldwin. "And keep an eye out for phantom clampers. Can I get you anything?"

"No thanks. I had a good breakfast."

Smith returned with two pies and a sausage roll. The pies were gobbled down before they'd even reached the road that led back to the station.

"That's better," he wiped the crumbs from the side of his mouth. "I'll save the sausage roll for later. What time is it?"

"Almost three," Baldwin replied. "We're going to be late."

"Detective work doesn't work to a strict timeline. Brownhill knows that and you'll learn it in time."

* * *

The look on Brownhill's face told a different story. The DI appeared far from impressed. She sat behind her desk with her hands clasped in front of her. "Nice of you to join us. Where have you been?"

"All over," Smith replied. "Gathering information. And to top it off, I had my car clamped."

"Nothing surprises me anymore. Can we make a start?"

Bridge and Yang Chu sat quietly on opposite sides of the room. Something was going on between them – they were obviously not speaking to each other. Smith sat next to Bridge. "Go ahead, boss," he said to Brownhill. "The floor's yours."

She opened up a file and took out some photographs. She handed one to each member of the team. "This is the photo-fit Katie Laing came up with of the man who killed Joy Williams."

Smith looked at the photograph. The man on the page didn't look like a deranged killer – he looked more like a mascot at a football game. His droopy eyes and upturned mouth made him look quite harmless."

"He looks like Yogi Bear," Bridge said. "Are you sure this Laing woman got it right?"

"Positive," Brownhill said. "She flinched when the photo-fit artist showed her the finished version. This is our killer. She described him as over six feet six and around twenty stone."

"A bloke like that wouldn't exactly be able to blend into a crowd," Yang Chu said.

Bridge snorted. "Duh. If you recall, I said that earlier. Try and keep up."

"I'm just pointing it out again. You were so hungover earlier, I wasn't sure if you'd remember saying it."

"I wasn't hungover. I could still give you a damn good…"

"You two," Brownhill shouted. "That's enough. Neither of you are helping here."

The room was silent for a moment. Bridge and Yang Chu both folded their arms and sat like petulant children. Brownhill turned to Smith. "This information you've been gathering – would you care to enlighten us?"

"We spoke to Joy Williams' boss. He didn't give us much as such – he'd only known her for a few years but he gave her the name of a bloke who knew her before that."

"And you think that'll help?"

"It can't hurt. What happened to these three women has something to do with being unworthy of something. I figure the best way to find out what that might be is by digging around in their respective pasts. Motive."

"The gospel according to Bob Chalmers?" Brownhill said.

"He's right. I've been thinking about the Joy Williams killing. Leaving the babysitter alive after letting her see his face was risky. I don't think he's going to show himself for a while. For all he knows, we could plaster that photo-fit all over the media."

"I still think we should," Bridge chipped in.

"I'm inclined to agree," Brownhill added.

"No," Smith said. "Not yet."

"Can I say something?" Baldwin said. "He knows the babysitter saw his face. He knows she can describe him. Surely he'll expect to see himself in all the papers soon."

"Not necessarily," Smith argued. "For all he knows, she could have been in such shock, she didn't remember anything."

"That's ridiculous," Brownhill said. "What exactly are you hoping to gain from this exercise, anyway?"

"Something links those three women together – there's something they all have in common and when we find out what that is we'll be closer to finding out why someone would want them dead."

"I still don't get why we can't put his description out there," Bridge said. "Someone must know who he is. That's how we'll catch him."

"I'm starting to see where Smith is going with this," Yang Chu said.

"Teacher's pet," Bridge scoffed.

"Bridge!" Brownhill said. "I said that's enough."

"He's going to be on his guard," Yang Chu continued. "He might even disappear altogether if he sees his face plastered all over the media. Then

we'll never catch him. Once we find out what these women have in common we can start looking in the right direction and catch this man off his guard."
"Precisely," Smith said.

"We'll hold off for two days," Brownhill conceded. "But on Saturday, I'm handing that photo-fit over to the press liaison officer. And God help us if there's another murder before that. If the media get wind that we had a description of the murderer and we held it back it'll be all our balls on the line."

"And what nice balls they are, boss," Smith said.

Yang Chu started to snigger. Even Bridge had a smile on his face.

"Here's the plan," Brownhill said. "Smith, you and Baldwin can speak to this man who knew Joy Williams before she started to work for Love IT. See if you can find anything that's relevant here. Bridge, I want you and Yang Chu to dig further into Julie Phelps' past."

Bridge glared at Yang Chu. "Do I have to work with him?"

"Yes you do. I'm going to see if Magda Collins has any skeletons in her closet that she's kept quiet all these years. Something ties these three women together and we're going to find out exactly what that is."

CHAPTER TWENTY NINE

Smith walked outside the station to find Bridge and Yang Chu involved in a heated argument. Voices were raised and Smith got the feeling that violence wasn't far off.
He stood between the red-faced DCs. "What the hell is going on between you two? If this is about the DS position neither of you are doing yourselves any favours."
"He's been here for five minutes," Bridge argued. "What gives him the right to even apply for it?"
"Because I'm a better man for the job," Yang Chu replied. "At least I don't stay out all night boozing it up."
"Only because you can't handle your drink. What kind of detective doesn't even drink?"
"One who's almost guaranteed the DS job."

Smith couldn't stop what happened next. He got out of the way just in time. Bridge swung a punch, Yang Chu ducked and Bridge's fist connected with fresh air. Smith tried to pull Bridge away but Yang Chu was too quick. First, it was a stomach jab with the left and then a full blown right hook hit Bridge on the side of the face."
"Stop it!" PC Baldwin had come outside to see what was going on. "Stop it right now. You'll both find yourselves unemployed if you keep this up. You'll shake hands right now and stop this nonsense."
Bridge held his hand to his sore cheek. "Not going to happen."
"Do it," Smith said. "And that's an order. From now on there'll be no more of this shit. You," he looked at Bridge. "Do yourself a favour and start spending more time swotting for the sergeant's exam and less time on drinking and womanising. And you," he addressed Yang Chu. "Stop winding him up. You

both have the potential to be bloody good detective sergeants. This territorial pissing stops right now. Have I made myself quite clear?"
Bridge, Yang Chu and Baldwin all looked at Smith with wide open eyes.
"Now that that's over with," Smith continued. "Let's get to work shall we? Bridge, put some ice on that cheek – I think you're going to have quite a bruise there in the morning."

"I can't believe they had a fist fight in the car park," Baldwin said as they drove away from the station. "They were like a pair of schoolboys."
"Let's hope they've got it out of their systems," Smith said. "We don't need that at the moment."
"Can I say something, Sarge?"
"Go ahead."
"You've changed."
"No I haven't."
"You have. You've grown up. I've watched you over the years and you've definitely grown up."
"I don't know whether to take that as a compliment or not."
"Take it as a compliment. Do you think Bridge and Yang Chu will stop their bickering now?"
"For a while. They're still young – their testosterone levels haven't quite evened out yet."
"Says the wise old man."
Smith started to laugh. "I'm past thirty. I have a child at home now. Can we change the subject? You're making me feel quite depressed. What was that address again?"

* * *

Bridge and Yang Chu didn't say a word on the way to John Phelps' house. Bridge was still nursing his sore cheek. Yang Chu parked next to the kerb and turned off the engine. They both got out of the car and walked up the driveway. Yang Chu shivered – the way his stomach had reacted when he first came here was still fresh in his mind. The vision of Julie Phelps' mashed up face still haunted him.

"Sorry about before," he said. "I really want that DS position."

"Me too," Bridge said. "Where the hell did you learn to fight like that?"

"As a Vietnamese bloke in the council estate where I grew up, it was a kind of a necessity."

"You much teach me some of those moves."

Yang Chu held out his hand. "Let's call a truce. May the best man win."

Bridge took the hand. "I'll drink to that. Or maybe not."

He knocked on the door. John Phelps answered moments later. He was holding Harry, his six month old son in his arms.

"Mr Phelps," Bridge said. "We're sorry to bother you but we need to ask you some more questions. Can we come in?"

"Of course," Phelps stepped aside. "I'll put the kettle on."

"Mr Phelps," Bridge began. He, Yang Chu and Phelps sat in the living room. Phelps had placed the baby on a blanket on the floor. "We need to ask you a bit more about Julie. I'm sure you're aware that two other women were killed this week and we believe it was the same killer."

Yang Chu leaned forward in his chair. "Do you know Magda Collins or Joy Williams?"

"No," Phelps replied. "I've never heard of them."

Harry started to cry on the floor. Phelps picked him up. "Sorry, it's time for his feed. I just need to warm up some formula."

He took the baby with him through to the kitchen.

"I'm never having kids," Bridge whispered to Yang Chu. "They're nothing but trouble."

"I think I'd like to have a few kids one day. Not yet, though. I'll wait until I'm a DCI first."

John Phelps returned before Bridge had a chance to reply to Yang Chu's comment. "Sorry, I'm not coping too well on my own at the moment. What do you want to know? I thought I'd told you everything."

"Mr Phelps," Yang Chu said. "We have reason to believe that Julie, Magda Collins and Joy Williams knew each other. Something connects them together."

"And we think that connection is why they were killed." Bridge added.

"I've never heard of Magda Collins or Joy Williams. Julie certainly didn't mention them, anyway."

"OK," Bridge could see they weren't getting anywhere. "When we spoke to you before you said that Julie was quite open about her past. Could you tell us a bit more about that?"

"She had a bit of a reputation. She wasn't proud of her past but she never denied the things she did. She changed – that's the important thing. She was a good mother and the best wife anybody could wish for."

"This reputation," Yang Chu said. "Could you elaborate?"

"She was a bit of a wild girl, that's all. She had quite a few men and she liked to drink a bit. Like I said, she put all that behind her – she even did a stint in rehab."

"Rehab?" Bridge said.

"It was before I met her. It worked. She stopped drinking altogether. Her life changed for the better. Until..."

"OK, Mr Phelps," Bridge nodded to Yang Chu to indicate it was time to leave and they both stood up at the same time. "Sorry to have to ask you all these questions again. We're going to find out who did this to your wife, I promise."

"A person's past shouldn't be allowed to come back and haunt them like this," Phelps slumped in his chair.

"We'll keep you informed of any breakthroughs in the investigation," was all Yang Chu could think of to say.

CHAPTER THIRTY

Smith had arranged to meet Eric Lee at an Internet café smack bang in the city centre. He was the man who recommended Joy Williams for the job with Love IT. As soon as he walked through the doors with Baldwin, Smith immediately felt out of place. He'd never been in an Internet café before and he was shocked at what he saw. The décor was ultra-modern, a counter ran along the whole of one wall – every booth was occupied by men and women – young and old. Most of them were wearing headphones. On the wall were framed photographs of people Smith didn't recognise. The café section occupied a tiny portion of the room and Smith noticed that very few of the patrons appeared to be eating or drinking anything.

"Are you lost?" a man who appeared to be in his early forties asked. "Eric Lee. I assume you're the detective who phoned earlier."

"Is it that obvious?" Smith said.

"We can talk at my booth. I was just about to take a break anyway."

He led them to the far corner of the room and managed to find two extra chairs.

"I've never been to one of these places before," Smith said as they sat down. "I'm surprised to find it so busy."

"People like the peace and quiet. I was shocked when I heard about Joy. She was quite an IT talent."

"How long have you known her?" Baldwin asked.

"We were at college together. That was about eight years ago. We kept in touch afterwards. She was a great girl."

"Can you think of anybody who could have done this to her?" Smith asked.

"Of course not," Lee replied straight away. "Joy was a lovely person. She wouldn't hurt a fly. That poor kid is going to have to grow up without a mother."

"Did you know the father of Joy's child?" Baldwin asked.

"We met once. Very briefly. It was just after Joy and he hooked up. I didn't like him at all."

"Why's that?" Smith said.

"I just got a bad vibe about him. I can't explain it. I suppose some people just give off that kind of negative energy. Do you think he might be involved somehow?"

Smith suddenly felt very stupid. He realised they hadn't even bothered to speak to Joy's ex. He made a mental note to bring it up in the next meeting.

"You said you knew Joy eight years ago?" he said. "What was she like?"

"She was quiet," Lee said. "And very studious. She got very good grades."

"And you can't think of anything that would make someone want to harm her?"

"Nothing. I wish I could be more help."

"What did Joy do after college?"

"I heard she got a job with a company that installs tracking devices into cars. I think that's where she met Fraser, the creep that got her pregnant."

"So her ex was into computers too?" Baldwin asked.

"He wasn't as good as he pretended to be. He was more into his alcohol than anything else. I don't know what Joy saw in him in the first place."

Smith's phone started to ring in his pocket. He took it out and looked at the screen.

"Hey, you." It was Whitton.

"There's someone in the back garden," Whitton sounded terrified.

Smith could hear dogs barking in the background.

"Where are the Theakston and Fred?"

"In the house with me and Laura."

"Lock all the doors. I'm on my way." Smith ended the call and ran out of the Internet café without any explanation to Baldwin and Eric Lee.

He drove his Ford Sierra far too quickly through the city. He narrowly missed a tourist bus that was turning onto Walmgate. He took the slip road and carried on at close to 100mph towards his house. He was out of the car before it had even come to a complete halt and he ran up the path. He took his keys out, opened the front door and closed it behind him. Whitton and Laura were in the kitchen looking out the window that faced onto the back garden. Theakston and Fred were sitting on the floor.

"Are they still there?" Smith asked Whitton.

"He jumped back over the fence," Whitton said. "He was huge."

"Lock the door behind me," Smith opened the kitchen door and went outside.

He noticed straight away that the fence at the back was damaged. It had been bent back in places. He approached it slowly. He was on his guard. He realised he ought to have told Bridge what was going on but all his thoughts were of Whitton and Laura. He peered over the fence and spotted the car about thirty metres to the right. One of its doors closed and it sped off down the access road. He took out his phone and called the switchboard at the station.

A man answered. "York City Police."

"This is DS Smith. I need all available cars to be on the lookout for a black Renault. I didn't get the license number but it's in the vicinity of Hale Road right now. This is extremely urgent."

Smith went back to the house and nodded to Whitton at the window to let her know she could open the door. He went inside and put his arms around her. "What happened?"

"I was just washing a few dishes when I spotted something at the end of the garden," she told him. "Something caught my eye. The next thing I know, this giant is making his way over the fence and the dogs are going crazy."

"It's alright. Whoever it was is long gone by now. I've put the word out. The traffic blokes have probably picked him up already. Come here."
He hugged her more tightly.
"What the hell is going on here?" Whitton broke the embrace.
"I don't know. Did you get a good look at the guy?"
"Not really. Apart from the fact he was built like a house. By the time I'd locked the kitchen door and phoned you, he'd legged it. Do you think it's the Unworthy killer?"
"Probably not," Smith tried to sound as convincing as possible but as soon as the words had left his mouth he knew he'd done a terrible job.
He turned on the kettle and made two cups of coffee. He set them down on the table and picked up Laura. She smiled at him – she appeared to be oblivious to what had just happened.

The noise of the front doorbell made everyone, including the two dogs jump. Smith walked through to answer it.
"Who is it?" he said through the letterbox.
"Brownhill. They found the car. Can you let me in?"
Smith unlocked the door and opened it.
"Is Whitton alright?" Brownhill asked."
"She's fine. Come in." Smith made another cup of coffee and handed it to the DI. "Where did they find the car?"
"About two miles from here on the Foss Road. It looks like it was abandoned."
"Do we know who it belongs to?"
"They're working on that as we speak." She turned to Whitton. "What happened?"
"A man broke into our garden," Whitton replied. "That's what happened. What the hell is going on here? If this is the Unworthy killer what was he doing in our garden?"

"We don't know for sure it's the same man," Brownhill sounded even less convincing than Smith.

"Of course it's the same man. How many six foot six brick shithouses are there in York? What does he want with me?"

"We don't know," Smith said. "You're safe now."

"I don't feel very safe."

Brownhill took out her phone. "Grant, I need you and your team at Smith's house as soon as possible." She rang off without further explanation.

"How did you get here so quickly?" Smith asked her.

"I was in the area," Brownhill replied. "I always have the radio switched on. When I heard the call-out, I came as soon as I could."

"I see," Smith said under his breath.

"What's that supposed to mean?"

"Nothing." Smith turned to Whitton. "This man – this giant, you said you didn't get a good look at him. Was there anything about him you remember? Facial features, hair colour, anything?"

"I've already told you everything I saw. I'm not an idiot and I don't appreciate this interrogation."

"I'm sorry but you know the drill."

"I know the drill alright. I'm sick of the bloody drill – I'm sick and tired of my life at the moment."

She picked Laura up and went upstairs.

"She'll be fine," Brownhill said. "She's had a bit of a shock, that's all. We'll catch this man."

"Since when did you listen in to the police radio?" Smith asked her. "I've never heard it before when I've been driving with you?"

"I'm a detective inspector, in case you've forgotten. It's my business to know what's going on at all times."

"If you say so."

A knock at the door put an end to the awkward silence that followed. Brownhill appeared to be relieved. "That'll be Grant. I'll let him in." Smith stood and watched her as she left the kitchen to let the head of forensics in.

Webber had brought two of his team with him. He nodded to Smith. "Webber," Smith said. "I'm not sure if you'll find much. Check the fence at the end of the garden."

He took out a cigarette, lit it and led Webber out into the back garden. Webber headed straight for the fence at the back. Smith followed closely behind him. "Since when did Brownhill start listening in to the police radio? She's never had it on when I've been driving with her."

Webber frowned. "She doesn't listen to it. Why would she? That's what mobile phones are for."

"That's what I thought. I'm going back inside the house. See if I can't calm Whitton down a bit."

CHAPTER THIRTY ONE

Whitton and Brownhill were sitting at the kitchen table when Smith went back inside. Theakston was on one side of Whitton's chair – Fred on the other. They appeared to be taking their guard duty very seriously.

"I'm sorry," Smith put his hand on Whitton's shoulder.

"It's not your fault," Whitton told him. "I don't know what's happening to me at the moment. I didn't think it was going to be this hard and this thing with the giant in the garden has really freaked me out."

Brownhill stood up. "I'll leave you to it. Is there somewhere you can stay tonight? I'm not sure it's a good idea to stick around here."

"Do you think he's going to come back?"

"I don't know but I'd rather you didn't take that risk."

"I'll be here," Smith pointed to the dogs. "And those two won't be easy to get past."

"It's just a suggestion. Let me know what you decide. I'll see myself out."

"She was acting a bit weird," Smith said when Brownhill was gone.

"What do you mean?" Whitton asked.

"I don't know. That stuff about listening in on the police radio. She got here within minutes."

"She's concerned, that's all. Do you think she was right about me not staying here?"

"Not at all. I'm not going to let you out of my sight. Let's talk about something else. You have a birthday coming up in case you've forgotten. I was thinking about having everyone around for a barbecue. What do you think?"

"Who's everyone?"

"Everyone. Bridge, Yang Chu, Baldwin. Even Brownhill and Webber. And Chalmers if that's alright. It'll take our minds off things. And you won't have to lift a finger – I'll organise everything."

"A good old-fashioned Aussie Barbie?"

"Something like that."

"I suppose it could be fun."

Smith's phone started to ring.

"Answer it," Whitton insisted.

It was Baldwin. "Is everything alright, Sarge?"

"It is now. I'm a bit tied up at the moment. What is it?"

"I didn't get much more out of Eric Lee. Joy Williams seems to be squeaky clean. I think we should speak to her ex, though. Fraser Jenkins. I got his details off the internet. He's still in York."

Smith looked at his watch. "It's late. We'll make an early start in the morning. I'm not leaving Whitton alone. Oh and, Baldwin, what are your plans for Saturday?"

"I've got no plans."

"Good. It's Whitton's birthday and we're all going to celebrate it in style."

He rang off without offering any further details. His phone rang again.

"Sarge," it was Bridge. "That car that was abandoned."

"Go on."

"It was reported stolen this morning."

"Great. That doesn't help much."

"I just thought you ought to know."

"Thanks, Bridge," Smith said and rang off.

    He walked down the hallway and locked the front door. He did the same at the back. He took two beers from the fridge, opened them both and handed one to Whitton.

"Right," he sat down next to her. "Do you feel like going over what we've got so far?"

Whitton smiled. "I thought you'd never ask. Shoot."

"Julie Phelps," Smith began. "26 years old. Mother of a six month old boy, Harry. She was the first one – her face was caved in with an electric iron. She was found by her neighbour when the baby wouldn't stop screaming. She was a bit of a wild one but according to her husband she'd calmed down since the baby came along. The word, Unworthy was written in blood on her back window. Forensics have shown that it was her blood. Feel free to interrupt me at any time."

"The iron," Whitton said. "Was it hers?"

"It was. Why do you ask?"

"Just bear with me. Her husband was away at the time, wasn't he?"

"Go on."

"Don't you think it strange that whoever killed her did it on a night when her husband was away?"

"You think he knew the husband wouldn't be there?"

"It looks that way."

Smith finished his beer in one go. "So it was carefully planned."

"And the electric iron?"

"If it was planned in advance, why kill her with something that was just lying around?"

"Exactly. Why leave it up to chance?"

Smith fetched two more beers from the fridge. "OK, we'll come back to that. Magda Collins – killed with a carving knife in her kitchen while her three year old, Jonathan was in the house. She was killed during the day."

"Do I have to ask if the knife was hers?"

"Shit. We didn't even think about the connection between the murder weapons. Both Julie Phelps and Magda Collins were killed with weapons this maniac found in their houses."

Laura was making low gurgling noises in the high chair opposite them.

"Do you have something to add?" Smith asked her. "Or do we have to leave it all up to your smart Alec mother to crack this one?"

Whitton started to laugh. "She's hungry. I'll leave you to digest what this lowly DC has told you while I fix her some milk."

Ten minutes later, Laura had finished the whole bottle and expelled a belch any beer-swilling Rugby player would be proud of.

"That child is a pig," Smith said. "Where were we?"

"The murder weapons. The third victim was strangled wasn't she?"

"Joy Williams," Smith said. "Strangled in front of her babysitter while her daughter was asleep in bed."

"He didn't need a weapon," Whitton said. "He intended to strangle all of these women. I read somewhere that in over 80% of cases involving male serial killers – they kill with their bare hands. It's supposed to be some kind of domination thing. In documented cases of serial killing where a woman is the murderer they almost always use a weapon. We know that he's incredibly strong. He didn't enter any of the houses with a weapon."

"Strangulation," Smith sighed. "I also read somewhere that unless you have the killer's hands to compare the bruise marks too, it's almost impossible to pull any evidence. At least with a knife or an iron we could've found some prints."

"You didn't find any though, did you?"

Smith suddenly remembered something. "He was wearing gloves. The bastard was wearing gloves. Webber mentioned about the word written on the window at Julie Phelps' place. He said the smudging was consistent with a gloved finger dipped in blood. The iron and the knife were probably at hand and he deemed them more convenient ways of killing somebody. God, I've missed you at work."

"Hold that thought. I need a pee."

"I'm going out for a smoke. Don't worry – I'll guard the door."

They sat back down at the kitchen table. Smith opened another beer. "OK, what we have so far are three unconnected victims. We've yet to find anything that links them together apart from the fact that all three are mothers of small children. As far as we know, they're from totally different backgrounds."

"Unworthy," Whitton said. "What were these women unworthy of?"

"I miss The Ghoul," Smith said out of the blue. "My head's spinning. This beer isn't helping. I need something to help me think."

"You're not smoking weed while we have the baby in the house."

Smith got up and returned with a bottle of Jack Daniel's. "I wasn't thinking about weed."

He poured two healthy measures and took a large sip. "Who, how, when and why? That's what The Ghoul always used to say. We've exhausted the when and the how – I don't think they're important."

"So focus on the who," Whitton said. "And the why will jump out at us sooner or later. What does Chalmers always go on about – motive?"

"We have been. Nothing so far links these three women together. Nothing at all. Julie Phelps was 26, Magda Collins, 30 and Joy Williams was 32."

"And I'm 28," Whitton mused.

"Excuse me?"

"He was here in our garden, remember?"

Smith finished the whiskey in his glass and poured himself another. "If it was the same guy, that part is a total mystery."

"It was the same guy," Whitton insisted. "What the hell was he doing here? What have I got to do with all of this?"

"This whole thing is messing with my head. We've got three dead women and we're still no closer to finding out who this lunatic is. I'm beginning to think that Bridge was right. We've got a description of the man – Bridge thinks we should put it out all over the media."

"And you disagree with him?"

"I'm having my doubts. I'm worried we'll scare him off and then we'll never catch him."

"So you'd rather wait until he does it again? It could have been me today." The thought made Smith feel sick to the stomach. Whitton was right. She could have easily been the fourth one.

Smith drained his glass and looked at the clock on the wall. It was almost midnight. "It's late. We should get to bed." He picked up Laura and grimaced. "I'll change her and bring her up. You know I'll never let anything happen to you don't you, Erica?"

CHAPTER THIRTY TWO

"We're going for a walk."
"It's late, Bee," the big man said. "I'm tired. What if someone sees us?"
"What if they do? Nobody will pay us any attention. Besides, we'll go somewhere quiet. I've been horrible to you, haven't I?"
"I don't want to go out, Bee. It's late."
"Please. We'll go somewhere nice. When was the last time we took a walk together down by the river? The boats are still there. We can go and look at the boats if you like."

The sun had set and the lights that lit up the bridge over the River Ouse were flickering over the dark, slowly flowing current. It was a warm, late September night but the path that followed the river was deserted apart from the odd couple who made their way away from the lights of the city.
"See," Bee said. "We've got the place to ourselves. I need to talk to you. Stop here."
They sat on the walkway on the bank of the river. The water oozed past their feet a few metres below.
"This is nice," the man admitted.
Bee put her arms round his huge shoulders. "I'm sorry. This is all my fault."
"It's not your fault, Bee."
"Yes it is."

She removed her hand from her brother's shoulder, slipped the knife from her pocket and stabbed him hard in the back of the neck. Before he realised what was going on, she'd shoved him with all her might. She was surprised when his huge bulk hardly made a sound as it hit the water below.

CHAPTER THIRTY THREE

The rain pelting down on the roof woke Smith from a dream about dogs. A pack of small dogs were chasing after a single, much larger one. One minute they'd be snapping their jaws at the tail of the monster canine but the next moment it would increase its speed and tear away into the distance. This happened four or five times before Smith finally woke up. He turned over in bed to find Whitton breathing heavily next to him. He forgot about the dream almost straight away. He slid out from under the duvet and checked on his daughter. Laura was also asleep. He left the ladies in peace and went downstairs to make some coffee. His mobile phone was lying on the kitchen table. He checked for messages and was pleasantly surprised when the screen was blank. Theakston and Fred arrived together and nudged at the back door to let Smith know they wanted to go outside.
"It's cats and dogs out there, guys," Smith told them. "You might want to take a couple of umbrellas with you."
He opened the door, the dogs went out and returned a few seconds later with expressions of utter disgust on their faces.
"I told you."

Smith boiled the kettle and made coffee. The rain was still hammering against the window. There was a thud in the hallway as the Friday newspaper fell onto the mat. Smith walked through to pick it up and opened the front door. The rain was falling away from the house – the doorway was sheltered so Smith took out his cigarettes and lit one. The road was drenched – it had obviously rained quite heavily during the night.
Autumns on the way, Smith thought and exhaled a huge cloud of smoke. Cars were driving slowly past the house – their windscreen wipers were finding it hard to keep up with the pelting rain. Smith finished his cigarette

and went back inside. The sound of the toilet flushing upstairs told him that Whitton was up and about.

"Laura's still asleep," Whitton walked in the kitchen. "I can't believe it – she slept through the whole night."

"It must be the rain," Smith suggested. "It's quite soothing. Coffee?"

"That would be great. What time do you have to be in this morning?"

"In about twenty minutes. This weather's going to slow things down for us."

"Welcome to Yorkshire."

Smith made some more coffee. "I'm just going to have a quick shower. My head's a bit tender. How much Jack did I have last night?"

"Pretty much all of it."

"Urgh," Smith said and went upstairs.

Whitton fetched the newspaper from the hall table. On the front page was a photograph of the River Ouse in full flow. The photograph was taken a few years back during the huge floods but, as Whitton read the article, experts were warning of a repeat performance.

"Great," Whitton said out loud. "That's all we need."

She stopped reading and took a sip of coffee. Smith's phone started to ring on the table. Whitton picked it up and looked at the screen – it was DI Brownhill. Whitton wondered whether to answer it but decided against it.

"Was that my phone?" Smith walked in. His hair was still wet from the shower.

"Brownhill," Whitton told him. "I ignored it."

"Good. I'd better go in and see what she wanted. Will you be alright here by yourself? Maybe you should think about what the DI suggested – maybe you should stay somewhere else until this all blows over."

"Where would I go? And what about you? I seem to remember you saying something about never letting anything happen to me."

"I won't. Just keep the doors locked and don't open them for anyone. OK?"

"Yes, Sarge. You're going to be late – you know how stroppy Brownhill gets when you're not on time."

Smith kissed her on the forehead. "I'll let you know if anything comes up. Lock the door behind me."

The rain was showing no sign of slowing down as Smith drove the few miles to the station. The sky was a murky brown colour and Smith knew that meant it would probably rain all day. He turned on his lights but they didn't seem to make any difference. He drove under thirty the whole way and was relieved when he turned into the car park at the station. He got out of the car and ran inside. Yang Chu and Bridge appeared to be sharing a joke by the front desk. The animosity between them seemed to have eased off for the moment.

"Morning," Smith addressed them both. "You two are in high spirits."

"DS rivalry," Bridge told him. "They've set a date for the sergeant's exam and we're just busy comparing irrelevant notes. Half of the stuff on the syllabus is gobbledygook."

"Typically, those in the best position to anticipate ethical challenges are…?" Yang Chu elaborated.

"Exactly," Bridge said. "What a load of bollocks. Ethical challenges – what the hell is that all about?" He looked at Smith. "What ethical challenges have you come across, Sarge?"

"When's the exam?" Smith ignored the question.

"The fourth of next month. Just under two weeks."

"Keep swotting. Where's the boss?"

"Brownhill?" Yang Chu said. "She's not in yet."

"That's odd," Smith said. "She phoned me this morning."

"What did she want?" Bridge asked.

"I was in the shower. I missed the call. I'm going to get some coffee from the canteen. If the DI doesn't show up soon, I'm going to start the briefing without her. We've got a lot to go through."

"We'll see you in the conference room," Bridge said.

Ten minutes later, Smith, Bridge and Yang Chu sat quietly in the small conference room. Baldwin and Brownhill had yet to show their faces. Smith looked at his watch. It was 7:30. "Where are those two?"

Right on cue, Brownhill and Baldwin walked in together. The DI looked liked she hadn't slept a wink – her hair was knotted and she had dark rings around her eyes. Baldwin, on the other hand looked fresh and bright-eyed.

"Sorry I'm late," Brownhill sat down at the head of the table. "Let's get started, shall we?"

"Are you alright, boss?" Smith asked her. "You look worse than me this morning."

"I'm fine. Right, let's go over what we have so far. Smith."

"Julie Phelps," Smith began. "26 years old. Killed with her iron at around ten at night. Her baby was screaming the whole time. She had a bit of a wild past but by all accounts, she'd calmed down a lot since her baby was born. Joy Williams. 32 years old."

"What about Magda Collins?" Bridge interrupted him. "Shouldn't we go through it in order? She was the second victim."

"No she wasn't." Smith glared at him. "She was the second one to be found but we have a witness who can tell us that Joy Williams was killed before Magda Collins. Can I carry on?"

"Sorry, Sarge."

"Joy Williams. Strangled in front of the babysitter. Small child asleep in the house." Smith looked directly at Bridge. "Magda Collins. 30 years old. Stabbed in her kitchen while her son looked on. We've yet to find a link to these three women apart from the fact that they all had young children. Does anybody have anything to add?"

Silence.

"I was afraid of that," Smith continued. "Whitton and me spoke about a few aspects of the murders last night and one thing strikes me as odd."

"What's that?" Brownhill asked.

"Two of the murders were carried out using weapons that just happened to be at hand."

"The iron and the bread knife," Brownhill said.

"Exactly. Don't you think it's a bit strange that this man goes to great lengths to plan these murders and then kills the women with random weapons?"

"He relies on his strength," Baldwin suggested. "We know he's a big man – he must be incredibly strong with it."

"It's a fair point," Brownhill admitted. "But I can't see how it has much relevance here."

"I just said it's odd, that's all."

"Well I can't see the point of spending valuable time on something you think is *odd*. Anything else?"

"Julie Phelps spent a bit of time in rehab." Yang Chu joined in. "Her husband told us. He reckons she got herself straightened out and hadn't touched a drop since."

"And Joy Williams' ex was a bit of an alkie according to the bloke we spoke to yesterday," Baldwin added.

"Eric Lee," Smith said. "What else did he say about Joy?"

"Nothing much."

"We'll interview the ex during the course of the day. Did you get his contact details?"

"Fraser Needham. Mr Lee gave us his last known address."

"You and Smith can go and speak to him after the briefing," Brownhill said. "Do we actually have anything at all that can get us moving forwards in this investigation?"

"Who, how, when and why?" Smith thought out loud. "We know the who, the how and the when, what we need to focus on is why? Why were these women selected? Motive. Something connects these women together and I'm damned if I can figure it all out."

"Speak to this Fraser character."

"What about me and Yang Chu?" Bridge asked.

"I think it's time this man's description was put out there. We can't hold off on it any longer. Have you been involved with the press liaison officer before?"

"Only once," Bridge said. "During that Jimmy Fulton mess."

"It'll be the first time for me," Yang Chu admitted.

"It'll be good experience for you," Brownhill said. "I'll set up a meeting. Henry Short is going to love you two. Anything else before we conclude the meeting?"

"One more thing," Smith said. "What's everybody doing tomorrow? It's Whitton's birthday and I was thinking about doing a barbeque."

"In this weather?" Bridge said. "It's pissing it down out there."

"It'll stop before tomorrow."

"We're in the middle of a murder investigation," Brownhill said. "I don't think now is the time to be throwing sausages on the fire."

"It'll do us all the world of good – refresh the brain cells." Smith smiled at Brownhill. "You and Webber are invited of course. I'm going to ask Chalmers if he wants to come, too."

"Just don't invite the Super," Bridge said. "I don't think I could put up with that idiot at a barbecue."

"That's settled then," Smith said. "Come on, Baldwin – let's see what this Fraser Needham bloke has to tell us."

"Smith," Brownhill said when everyone was ready to leave. "Can I have a word in private?"

"What's up, boss?"

Brownhill waited for Bridge, Yang Chu and Baldwin to leave the conference room and closed the door.

"What's going on?" Smith asked her.

"I'm afraid this can't be overlooked. You mentioned in the briefing that you've been discussing matters pertaining to this investigation with your girlfriend."

"Otherwise known as DC Whitton," Smith pointed out.

"Be that as it may, DC Whitton is not working on this case, nor is she actually a current member of this team. She's on maternity leave and as such she has no right to be privy to information regarding this case."

Smith couldn't believe what he was hearing.

"Are you being serious? Whitton has been involved in just about every successful murder investigation we've had. She's a bloody good detective."

"I'm not doubting her competence – I'm merely pointing out that you have no right to be blurting out every aspect of this investigation willy-nilly. I suggest you pick another topic of conversation for your pillow talk."

Smith could feel his face getting hotter and hotter. He glared at Brownhill, stood up and left the room.

He found Chalmers outside in the doorway smoking a cigarette.

"Morning, boss. Lovely day."

"Yorkshire," Chalmers handed Smith his packet of cigarettes. "Just how I like it. I believe you've got bugger all on this Unworthy thing."

Smith took out a cigarette and lit it. "Thanks. I need one of these right now. We've got nothing. We can't seem to find a connection between these three women. Me and Baldwin are off to speak to the ex of one of them now. Can I ask you a question? Two actually."

"Go on."

"What are you doing tomorrow afternoon? I'm thinking of doing something for Whitton's birthday. I'd like it if you could come."

"Free food?"

"Of course."

"Then I'll be there. What was the other question?"

"I've just had a bollocking from the DI for talking to Whitton about the ongoing investigation. Brownhill reckons I shouldn't tell Whitton what's happening at work. She reckons Whitton's not privy to that information whatever the hell that means."

"She's pissing on her territory," Chalmers finished his cigarette and lit another. "Stamping down her authority. Bryony's the kind of woman who has to let you know who's boss every now and then. I wouldn't even worry about it."

"Whitton's a brilliant detective."

"We all know that, the DI included – just don't let on you're discussing it with Whitton and everything will be fine. I'd better get back in. There's a stack of paperwork on my desk that just keeps getting bigger and bigger. Don't worry about Brownhill – you should know what she's like by now. What time tomorrow?"

"Boss?"

"This thing for Whitton."

"Around two."

"Great – I'll bring a nice bottle of scotch."

CHAPTER THIRTY FOUR

"What did the DCI say?" Baldwin asked Smith as they drove.
The rain was still pelting down on the windscreen.
"Chalmers will be there," Smith said. "He never could turn down a free feed. I just hope this weather calms down a bit for tomorrow."
"They're predicting floods again. As bad as the ones we had a few years ago, they reckon."
"Then we'll do something inside. Whitton deserves a good birthday bash. She's been going crazy at home all day with Laura."
"When do you think she'll be back at work again?"
"Not for a while. What's this address again?"
"Green Street – number 34."

The rain was starting to slow down. Smith could see a patch of blue sky in the distance.
Floods, my arse, he thought. *The weathermen have got it wrong again.*
Number 34 Green Street was a three storey terraced house that had been converted into flats. Fraser Needham rented the ground floor flat. He answered the door straight away in a sweatshirt and a pair of filthy tracksuit bottoms. Smith could smell the booze on his breath before he even opened his mouth – it was only just after 8 in the morning but he reeked of alcohol.
"Mr Needham?" Smith said.
"That's me. Got a computer problem?"
"Not exactly. DS Smith and this is PC Baldwin. Can we come in?"
"You got any ID? You can't be too careful these days. You could be planning on robbing me."
Smith took out his ID. Baldwin did the same. "Can we come inside, Mr Needham?"

Fraser Needham led them inside and closed the door behind them. "You'll have to excuse the mess. The cleaning lady didn't show up this morning." He smiled as if he'd made a huge joke and revealed a rotten set of teeth.

He opened the door to his flat and the stench hit Smith like a thick fog of foul gas. Baldwin grimaced at the noxious odour.

"Take a seat," Needham said. "Do you want something to drink?"

"No thanks," Smith and Baldwin said in unison.

Smith couldn't see anywhere to sit down that wouldn't risk contaminating his clothing – there were three heavily stained armchairs and two wooden dining room chairs that appeared to have three weeks worth of food caked on the seats.

How can people live like this? he thought.

He remained standing. "Mr Needham, we're here to talk to you about Joy Williams. I believe you and Joy were together for a while?"

"Stuck up cow," Needham said. "What's she said I've done? She thinks she's some big-shot now she works for that Love prat. I was the one who got her into this game. I introduced her to all my contacts. What's she accusing me of?"

"Nothing," Smith said. "She's dead."

Needham didn't seem to grasp what Smith had told him. His expression was one of utter confusion. "Dead?"

"I'm afraid so," Smith said. "You didn't know?"

"No I didn't know. I need a drink."

He walked over to a rusty refrigerator and took out a bottle of white wine. He took a long swig straight from the bottle.

"Dead?" he said again. "What happened?"

"She was found in the park yesterday morning," Baldwin told him. "She'd been strangled."

He took another long swig from the bottle. "You can't... You don't think I had something to do with it, do you?"

The acrid smell in the flat was starting to make Smith feel light headed. "We don't think anything at the moment, Mr Needham. Look, we need to speak to you and I'm sure you'll agree that this isn't the ideal place to do so. What I would like you to do is come with us to the station and we can have a more formal chat there. A shower and a change of clothes wouldn't be a bad idea. And please put down that bottle of wine – it's barely eight in the morning. You've got half an hour. We'll be waiting in the car outside. Come on, Baldwin."

He turned and left the flat before Fraser Needham had a chance to argue.

"My God, that place stinks," Baldwin said as they emerged into the fresh air. "I thought I was going to throw up in there."

The rain had stopped now and the clouds were disappearing towards the west. Smith took out a cigarette and lit it.

"He's obviously so used to it he doesn't even notice it anymore."

"Do you think he'll come with us? We've got nothing on him to arrest him."

"I didn't leave him much choice."

Smith's phone started to ring. He looked at the screen and his heart started to beat faster. It was Whitton.

"Is everything alright?" he answered it.

"Everything's fine," Whitton replied. "The DI's on her way here. She said she wanted to speak to me."

"Crap. I let it slip that you and me were discussing the investigation last night."

"So what?"

"She reckons you shouldn't be privy to that kind of information while you're on maternity leave. Her words, not mine."

"She sounded fine on the phone – pleasant even. I think what happened yesterday just got her worried. She probably just wants to check up on me. I think it's quite sweet."

"Sweet is not a word that will ever be used in the same sentence as Bryony Brownhill, Whitton."

"Where are you now?"

"We're bringing in Joy Williams' ex. His flat smells worse than a sewer so, for the sake of our nostrils, we're going to talk to him down at the station – not that you're privy to such information. He's coming out now. I'd better go. Give Bryony my love."

Whitton started to laugh. "I will. I'll see you later."

"Oh, Whitton, your birthday barbecue is on. Chalmers is coming too."

"I'll see you later."

Fraser Needham had changed into a slightly cleaner pair of tracksuit bottoms and a Black T-Shirt. A musty odour still lingered when he got in the car but it was nowhere near as bad as the stench inside his flat. Smith opened all the windows and turned the key in the ignition. They drove in silence for a while. Smith breathed in the fresh air the rainfall had left behind. He wondered why Brownhill had decided to pay Whitton a visit. The DI very rarely made house calls to her team and in light of the dressing down he'd received earlier in the conference room, something seemed odd about the visit.

"Why would someone want to kill Joy?" Needham broke the silence.

"We're not sure yet," Baldwin replied. "That's why we need your help."

"I didn't kill her, you know."

"We're not saying you did," Smith said. "We'll ask the questions at the station if you don't mind. Would you like us to call someone for you? Do you have legal representation?"

"Do I need a lawyer?"

"You're entitled to have legal representation with you when we interview you," Baldwin told him.

"I haven't done anything. I don't have a lawyer."

"We can provide one for you," Smith said. "But it could take a few hours to arrange."

"I haven't done anything," Needham said again. "I don't think a lawyer is necessary."

Smith stopped the car by the entrance of the station and all three of them got out. "This way," he led Needham inside and headed for the interview rooms.

He turned on the recording device. "Interview with Fraser Needham commenced - 9:05. Present DS Smith and PC Baldwin. Mr Needham has waived his right to legal representation. Mr Needham, you were in a relationship with Joy Williams a while back. Could you tell us about it?"

"We met at college. We were both doing some of the same IT modules and we hit it off straight away."

"How long were you and Joy together?" Baldwin asked.

"A couple of years, maybe three. When I finished my course I landed a position with one of the top IT companies in the North. Like I told you before, I was the one who introduced Joy to the people who count in this business – people who can make things happen."

"Are things still happening for you, Mr Needham?" Smith recalled the squalid flat he called home. "What about Rose, the child you and Joy had together? Aren't you in the least bit concerned that she was in the room next door whilst her mother was being strangled?"

"Rose ceased to be my problem when Joy told me to get the hell out her life."

"And you let her bring up your daughter alone?" Baldwin asked.

"It was Joy's choice. She made it very clear that I was to stay well away."

"OK," Smith realised this line of questioning wasn't getting them anywhere. "Let's go back to after you finished your course at college – you said you landed a position at a top IT company. Tell us about that."

"It was going well until I got mixed up with the wrong crowd. I started drinking heavily a while back and I haven't seemed to be able to stop. I'll get my life sorted out sooner or later. I still have it up here." He tapped his forehead.

"OK," Smith said. "You and Joy were together for a few years. In that time can you think of anyone who might have wanted to harm her?"

"Joy? Of course not. She got a bit too big for her boots when she landed that job with Love IT but she wasn't nasty about it."

"This wrong crowd you mentioned. Was Joy part of that crowd?"

"For a while. But she soon kicked them into touch."

"And I suppose you were non-too pleased about it?"

"Of course I wasn't. But I wouldn't do anything to hurt her if that's what you're thinking. I'm not a violent bloke – IT's my thing, not killing people."

Smith was inclined to agree. Fraser Needham didn't look like the kind of man who could harm anyone.

"OK, Mr Needham," he said. "Let's go back to this crowd of people you used to hang around with – the people you used to drink with. Can you think of anyone from that crowd who might have borne a grudge? You said that Joy soon kicked them into touch."

"We were mostly college students. None of the old crowd really cared when she stopped hanging out with them. There were always plenty more where she came from. Oh, she enjoyed it for a while – the late nights partying and drinking, but she soon decided that kind of life wasn't for her and she stopped. With a bit of help though."

"What do you mean?" Baldwin asked.

"Joy always had to do things properly. She was just like that. She realised she was heading down the wrong path and checked herself into a rehab place a few miles north of the city somewhere. I think that's actually where she found out she was carrying the kid. Two weeks was all it took and that was it – goodbye old life, hello new beginnings."

CHAPTER THIRTY FIVE

Henry Short had been a press liaison officer for twenty five years. In those years his job description had changed drastically and with the onset of digital media, Henry now coordinated the majority of his assignments from home. He led Bridge and Yang Chu through to a small, neat office he'd set up in one of the spare rooms in his house.

"Bryony has briefed me," he said. "Please take a seat. Can I get you gentlemen anything to drink before we begin?"

"No thanks," Yang Chu said.

Bridge wasn't paying attention. He was taking a particular interest in a photograph on the wall. It was a black and white photo of a young woman. She appeared to be in her early twenties and she was shown in profile.

"That's my daughter," Henry had noticed Bridge's keen interest.

"She's very pretty," Bridge said.

"She gets it from her mother. She's married to a boxer – heavyweight. Can we get cracking? I don't know how much you've had to do with the press in recent years but I can tell you that things have changed since I started out in this game. In the old days, my job was to act as a go-between between the police and the press, which back then consisted of real people. Nowadays, I very rarely deal with a face or a voice on the phone – it's all done on here." He tapped a few keys on his laptop.

"You're probably wondering why it's really necessary to employ somebody like to me to act as a go-between – why not just put the press statements out yourselves and save the bother and expense of a liaison officer? Let me tell you this. There are ways to deal with the media and there are ways not to. One false move and – boom, there goes the reputation of the police force in one fell swoop. Am I going too fast for you?"

This guy loves the sound of his own voice, Bridge thought.

"Not at all," he said. "Go on."

"Bryony explained to me that you have a description of a man you are looking for in connection with the three women who were murdered this week?"

"That's right," Yang Chu replied.

"A witness photo-fit?"

"Right again."

"And if it were up to you, how would you proceed with this?"

"Plaster his ugly mug all over the papers," Bridge said straight away. "Somebody must know who he is. Simple as that."

"Simple as that?" Henry smiled.

"That's right. Put his description on the front page of as many newspapers as we can and we'll catch him."

Henry scratched at a scab on his chin. "I see. From what I've gathered from the information that has been given to me, this investigation is rather delicate if I can put it like that. The York police believe this man is responsible for targeting women with small children."

"He believes them to be unworthy of something," Bridge added.

"That part cannot become public knowledge at this stage."

"Why not?"

"My job is not only to inform the general public of certain aspects of police cases – it is also to allay any panic that the knowledge of these aspects may cause to arise."

"Once more in English, please."

"Remember the Harlequin investigation," Yang Chu translated. "The press got wind of what was going on and we had a riot on our hands."

Bridge could hardly forget it – it was his loose tongue that had caused the news to get out in the first place.

"Then why do you need us here?" Bridge asked. "You obviously know what you're doing. We could be out trying to catch this maniac instead."

"Bryony wanted me to keep you in the loop – the local papers and even some of the bigger dailies will want to speak to a real person. Once this man's face hits the media, questions are going to be asked. Some of them will be tough to answer but I want to give you a heads up on what you can and can't tell the press."

"So we don't mention the *Unworthy* part," Bridge said.

"The fact that this person leaves something of a calling card at the crime scenes will suggest to the general public that a serial killer is at large and we want to avoid that at all costs."

Bridge shook his head. "Even if they don't know about the *Unworthy* part, surely it's already got out that all three victims had small children?"

"Half of the women in York have small children. I can't see many people putting two and two together. That's all for now. I have the photo-fit of the man in question. I'll be in touch if I need anything further from you. I have to warn you though – when this man's face does hit the mass media, it's not going to be pleasant for you. People are going to want results and they're going to want to know what the police are doing to catch this man. It's not going to make the force in general very popular."

"I didn't join up to win any popularity contests," Yang Chu said.

* * *

"That was a complete waste of time," Bridge said as they drove away from Henry Short's house. "He was a real nutcase if you ask me."

"He had a few valid points," Yang Chu argued. "We have to tread very carefully where the public are concerned. They'll be watching us like hawks once this goes viral."

"The world's gone mad," Bridge scoffed just as his phone started to ring in his pocket. He took it out and answered it.

"Bridge," it was Smith. "Where are you?"

"We've just finished up with the press guy. What's wrong?"

"Baldwin and me spoke with Joy Williams' ex boyfriend and we're on our way to speak with Julie Phelps' husband. We might just have found out what links these women together."

"A link?"

"Joy and Julie both spent time in rehab for alcohol addiction. We got the name of the centre Joy was at – it's a place about ten miles north of here. I need you to get hold of Magda Collins' brother, James and check to see if Magda was admitted too. This could be the break we've been waiting for."

"Rehab?" Bridge repeated.

"That's right. Get onto it. I want to call an emergency briefing back at the station at three. I need answers before then."

He rang off.

"What was that all about?" Yang Chu asked.

"Smith seems to think he's found a link between two of the dead women – they both spent time in rehab."

"Rehab?"

"They were alkies. The Sarge wants us to check out to see if Magda Collins spent any time there."

"Rehab," Yang Chu said again. "What if they did all spend time in rehab? That's hardly a motive for murder is it?"

"It's a lead and it's the only lead we have at the moment."

CHAPTER THIRTY SIX

John Phelps was still in his dressing gown when he answered the door to Smith and Baldwin. He held his son, Harry in his arms.
"Mr Phelps," Smith said. "Sorry to bother you again but some new information has come to light. Can we come in?"
"New information?" Phelps's eyes widened. "What new information?"
"Can we talk inside?"
"I was just busy making Harry's breakfast. Come through. I won't be a minute. Would you like something to drink?"
"No thanks," Smith said. "This shouldn't take long."
"Go through to the living room. This little bloke gets irritable when he's hungry."

Smith and Baldwin waited in the living room. The room was spotless – there was no indication that a brutal murder took place there only days earlier. Smith looked out of the window. The sky was clear and the rain that had pelted down earlier had disappeared completely.
"Sorry about that," John Phelps sat down on a single armchair. "What's this all about?"
"Mr Phelps," Smith began. "You mentioned earlier about Julie spending time in a rehabilitation centre for alcohol addiction."
"That's right. What's that got to do with anything?"
"Can you remember which centre it was?"
"It was some place about ten miles from the city. I can't remember the name off-hand."
"Please, Mr Phelps," Baldwin urged. "This could be important."
Smith decided to elaborate. "Joy Williams, one of the other women who was killed also did a stint inside rehab. It sounds like she could have been at the same place as Julie. It's something that links them both together."

"So they both spent some time getting cleaned up," Phelps said. "Why would that make someone want to kill them?"

"That's what we need to find out," Smith replied.

Phelps stood up. "Hold on." He left the room without further explanation.

He returned some time later with a flip file. He started to leaf through the pages. "Here we go." He showed the page to Smith.

"Weldon Rehabilitation Centre," Smith read out loud.

"It's just up the A64 outside Kirkham," Phelps elaborated. "According to the map."

"Can we borrow these records?" Smith asked. "We'll make copies and get them back to you as soon as possible."

"Keep them. I don't want them. Why would I want to be reminded of Julie's time in rehab? There are much fonder memories of her I'd like to concentrate on."

"We won't take up any more of your time. Thank you – you've been a great help."

"Do you think you'll catch him? Do you think you'll catch this bastard who did this to my Julie?"

"We'll do everything we can. I promise."

"Well, if you do, keep him away from me. I'm not a violent man but I think I'd probably kill him with my bare hands."

"We'll be in touch, Mr Phelps. Come on, Baldwin."

* * *

A few miles away Bridge and Yang Chu were having less luck with James France, Magda Collins' brother. France was refusing to tell them anything.

"My sister is barely cold and you come harassing me about some rehab centre. This is an outright insult."

"Please, Mr France," Bridge said. "This is extremely important. We've had some new information that could prove to be the link between two of the victims."

Smith had phoned Bridge as soon as he and Baldwin had finished talking to John Phelps.

"Julie Phelps and Joy Williams both spent time in the same rehabilitation centre," Yang Chu elaborated. "We need to find out if Magda also spent time there. It's a place called Weldon, just outside of Kirkham."

"It's just up the road on the A64," Bridge added.

"I know where Kirkham is. And I know nothing about any rehab centre there. I think it's time I phoned my lawyer again."

Smith had warned the two DC's to tread carefully with James France.

"Mr France," Bridge said. "We understand how difficult this is for you but you must understand it from our point of view – this is the first possible link to the three women who were killed and the sooner we establish all the facts, the sooner we can move forward with this investigation. We all want the same thing here."

"We want to catch whoever did this to your sister," Yang Chu said.

France didn't say anything. He scratched his head and seemed to be deep in thought.

"Is this going to get out?" he asked eventually. "About the rehab centre, I mean?"

"There's no reason why it should," Yang Chu assured him. "Do you know something?"

"You two make quite a double act. Do they teach you this sort of thing in Police College?"

"We make most of it up as we go along," Bridge admitted.

France rested his chin on his hands. "Magda did go away for a while," he sighed. "That's what we called it. She simply went away for a few months.

Mother wouldn't hear any different. I mean – an alcohol rehabilitation centre, it's hardly something you brag about, is it?"

"It's nothing to be ashamed of," Yang Chu assured him. "You should be proud your sister admitted she had a problem and did something about it."

"Anyway, it was long before she met Hugh, her late husband. She went through a bit of a rough patch – got mixed up with a bad lot and things spiralled out of control. Mother wanted nothing to do with her so she came to live with me for a while. The rehab centre was my idea. I gave her an ultimatum – either she got her act together or she was on her own. She was in the centre for a month."

"When was this?" Yang Chu asked.

"Mother died the year after so it will have been 2010. Sometime in the autumn. Are you sure this isn't going to get out?"

"We'll do our best to keep it quiet," Bridge promised him.

CHAPTER THIRTY SEVEN

Brownhill parked outside Smith and Whitton's house but didn't get out of the car. She sat for a while just staring out of the window in front of her. Her phone started to ring. She took it out and looked at the screen. It was Grant Webber. She let it go straight to voicemail. She took a deep breath and opened the car door. The rain had stopped and white clouds were forming in the sky. She walked up the path and knocked on the door. Whitton answered straight away.

"Are you alright?" she asked the DI. "You look quite pale."

"I didn't sleep much last night. A cup of strong coffee wouldn't go amiss." Whitton led her inside and locked the door behind them. "Orders from the boss. Smith has told me to keep the doors locked until this is all over."

"Where's the baby?"

"Sleeping. Laura's been quite a pleasure recently. She eats, sleeps and that's pretty much it. We've been lucky. I'll stick the kettle on."

They sat at the kitchen table. Brownhill sipped her coffee. Neither of them spoke for a few seconds.

"You said you wanted to speak to me," Whitton broke the silence.

"Did I? Oh, I just wanted to come and check to see if you were alright. That episode the other day must have rattled you a bit."

"I still can't believe it – he was in our garden. It was lucky we were all inside with the door locked. How are things going with the investigation?"

"You tell me," Brownhill raised her eyebrows. "Smith informs me that he's been discussing the case with you in some detail."

"I wouldn't put it like that – we have spoken about certain aspects but he's just keen to keep me in the loop."

"You're not officially at work, Erica."

Whitton flinched at the mention of her first name. The DI never called her by her first name.

"I know you were part of the team," Brownhill continued.

"I'm still part of the team," Whitton said. "I'm just on leave at the moment. Are you saying that I'm not allowed to offer my input?"

"I'm just saying it might be better if you concentrated on the reason you're actually on leave in the first place. That baby needs you full-time."

"Have I just been given a bollocking in my own home?"

"Of course not. I've said what needed to be said. Let's talk about something else. This coffee is delicious."

Whitton made another two cups of coffee. "Do *you* ever want kids?"

Brownhill's face turned even paler. She picked up her coffee and took a long sip. "Not all of us are cut out to have children. That's just the way it is."

"Rubbish. I never thought I'd be a mother one day but I'm loving it. There are bad days, of course but the feeling you get sometimes when you look into the eyes of something you've brought into the world has to be experienced to be believed."

"I can't have kids," Brownhill came straight out with it. "Like I said, that's just the way it is."

"I'm sorry. I didn't know. I'm so sorry."

"Don't be – I've learned to live with it. Besides, I don't really think I'm mother material."

"Why can't you have kids?"

"It's a long story. A story I don't feel like telling right now. It sounds like your breaks over."

The sound of a baby crying could be heard on the baby monitor on the table. Whitton stood up. "She'll just be hungry, and she probably needs changing. I won't be a minute."

She returned a few minutes later with Laura in her arms. The baby stared at Brownhill curiously. Whitton placed her in her chair and made her some formula.

"How old is she now?" Brownhill asked.

"Six months."

"She drinks like a fish."

Laura was halfway through the milk formula.

Whitton laughed. "She gets that from her dad."

"Are you planning on having any more?"

"Not in the near future. One's enough for now. I was an only child and I did just fine. Do you have any brothers or sisters?"

The DI stared vacantly out the back window into the garden. "I had a brother but he died. He was two years younger than me. I've got a photograph here somewhere."

She opened up her bag and fished out a crumpled photo. On it was a much younger looking Brownhill and a fat boy. He appeared to be around fifteen years old.

"His name was Warren," she said. "He was very big for his age."

"How did he die?" Whitton said. "If you don't mind me asking."

"Of course not. It was a long time ago. He was a big kid but his immune system was weak. He contracted meningitis and couldn't fight it off."

"I'm so sorry," Whitton said for the second time in the space of ten minutes.

"Don't be. Like I said, it was a very long time ago. I don't even know why I'm telling you all of this. I haven't really spoken about it to anybody – I haven't even told Grant about it. He knows I can't have children but he knows nothing of Warren. I really ought to be going. It's made a nice change to sit down and chat with another woman. We must do this again some time. I'll see myself out – you see to that beautiful lady of yours and make sure to lock the door behind me."

* * *

Smith turned right onto the A64 and headed north in the direction of Kirkham. The case meeting he'd scheduled earlier was going to have to do without him. He'd dropped Baldwin off at the station and she was to go through the events of the meeting with him later. He wanted to get everything in order today so the barbeque he was planning for Whitton could go ahead. He realised they couldn't really afford to take a day away from the investigation but he'd convinced himself they would be able to think more clearly after a day off.

This barbeque is just what everyone needs.

He'd arranged to meet with Kelly Bowen, the director of the Weldon Centre in Kirkham. He'd explained the circumstances and Kelly had been more than accommodating. He glanced at the sign on the side of the road. The Lemonwood hospital was only half a mile on the left.

What the hell, he thought and slowed down slightly, *I can kill two birds with one stone.*

Smith found Jessica Blakemore outside on one of the wooden benches. She was smoking a cigarette and writing something in a small notebook. He walked over to her. "Jessica. Sorry to come without making an appointment first. What have you got for me?"

Jessica looked up from her book. "If you'd made an appointment I'd think there was something wrong. Have a seat."

"What have you got for me?" Smith asked again.

"I've given it some thought," she leafed through the notebook. "You still haven't given me much to go on but from the first three murders it's clear that the Unworthy part is the key. Has he killed again?"

"No. Since the woman was found strangled in the park, there haven't been any others. He turned up at my house."

"He did what?"

"Whitton was inside with Laura and the dogs and he jumped over the fence and approached the house. Luckily the doors were locked."

"And you're sure it was the same man?"

"We compared footprints. It was our guy?"

"He was taking a huge risk trying to break into the house of the DS who's heading up the investigation. Why do you think he did that?"

"I was hoping you would tell me."

"I'm a shrink, Jason – I'm not a magician. What else can you tell me?"

"We found a link between the three dead women. All three of them spent time in a rehab centre not far from here. I'm actually supposed to be on my way there now."

"But you thought you'd make a slight detour? Rehab – that's interesting."

"I'm glad you find it interesting. We have the link but it still doesn't help us work out why these three women were killed."

"And what's Whitton got to do with it?" Jessica appeared to be lost in thought. "Did the mother of your child also spend time in a rehab centre?"

"Of course not."

"Have you asked her?"

"Whitton isn't a recovering alcoholic," Smith insisted.

Jessica took out another cigarette and lit it.

"When did you start smoking?" Smith asked her.

"It helps me to think." She handed him the lit one and lit another for herself.

"Let's go through this again. The first woman was killed at home."

"Julie Phelps," Smith said.

"Their names are not important. She had her face caved in with an electric iron didn't she? The other two were also killed in their homes. That implies careful planning. This man seems to know what he's doing. The only loose end is the babysitter. Why did he leave her alive after she'd seen his face?"

"We can't figure that one out," Smith admitted.

"A man kills three women. Their children are in the house while he does it. He leaves the children unharmed. At one of the murder scenes he leaves a witness behind. I'm afraid this one has me stumped."

"You're losing your touch."

"No, you are. Let me know how it goes at the rehab centre and get in touch then. There's no need to come here – you have my mobile number. I've got a consultation with another patient here in five minutes. I'll phone you if I think of anything else in the meantime."

CHAPTER THIRTY EIGHT

Smith parked outside the address Kelly Bowen had given him. The Weldon rehabilitation centre wasn't exactly what he was expecting. He thought it would be some kind of hospital building but the structure under the sign looked more like an exclusive office park. He made his way through the revolving doors at the entrance and approached the reception desk. The man behind it stood up and offered a sympathetic glance.
"Good afternoon, sir," he said. "How can I help you?"
"I have an appointment with Kelly Bowen," Smith took out his ID. "DS Smith."
"Ah yes. Miss Bowen did mention something about it. She's in a group therapy session at the moment. I'll take you through to her office – you can wait for her in there."
He led Smith down a corridor and stopped outside a white door. "Please go in. Would you like something to drink? Coffee? Tea?"
Smith felt like a beer. He was in an alcohol rehabilitation centre and the first thing to come to mind was a cold beer.
"Coffee would be great," he said. "Milk, no sugar."

He sat down on an expensive looking leather couch and scanned the room. Behind the desk on the wall hung various diplomas and certificates. The desk itself was free of clutter. A laptop computer and a photograph of a woman on a horse were all it had on it. The man from reception returned and handed Smith a mug of hot coffee.
"Miss Bowen will be here shortly," he said and left the room.
Smith thought about what he hoped to gain from being there. Three women had been killed and all of them had spent time in the centre. Why were these three women selected?

"Sorry to keep you waiting," a woman in her mid-thirties entered the room and sat down behind the desk. She was wearing a black sweater and a pair of black jeans. Her face was extremely pale and the black clothing only accentuated her pallor. Smith could see straight away that she wasn't the woman in the photograph on the desk.

"Please pull up a chair," she said. "I must admit, I was very intrigued by your phone call – and slightly disturbed I may add."

Smith sat opposite her. "Thank you for your time, Mrs Bowen. I'll try not to keep you any longer than necessary."

"Miss," she corrected him. "It's Miss Bowen."

"Miss Bowen. As I explained on the phone, three women who spent time at the centre in autumn 2010 were killed this week. Julie Phelps, Magda Collins and Joy Williams. Do you remember any of these women?"

"Of course. I make a point of remembering all of our guests here – especially those who leave here and make positive changes in their lives."

"The success stories, you mean?"

"Please don't be pedantic, detective. It's not an attractive trait in a man."

Smith wished he'd kept his mouth shut. "Sorry, so you still recall these three women after almost six years?"

"Let me explain something to you. Weldon is not a hospital – we like to think of it more as a wellbeing centre for those who have lost their way. Alcohol addiction isn't anything to be ashamed of. Sometimes circumstances change for the worse and alcohol is a way out. I'm sure you're not here to discuss the ins and outs of a rehabilitation centre – I have a budget meeting in half an hour so could you please get to the point."

"Certainly. These three women were all here at the same time. That's more than just a coincidence. What I need from you is a list of all the patients who were here in the autumn of 2010 and I also need to know who would have access to that list."

"I'm afraid that's out of the question. Here at Weldon, we value our guests' privacy. Confidentiality is paramount to our philosophy."

Smith had been afraid of this. "I appreciate what you're saying but, firstly, the privacy of these patients will not be compromised. You have my word that none of this information will be made public. Secondly, I believe that unless I have access to that list, somebody else on it is going to be the next one to be killed."

It was a cheap shot but it appeared to have the desired effect. Kelly Bowen glanced at the photograph on her desk and scratched her chin. "Do you really believe that the time these women spent here at Weldon has something to do with why they were killed?"

"It's the only link we've got so far," Smith admitted. "Please, Miss Bowen. I need that list. I wouldn't ask if it wasn't important."

Kelly Bowen opened up her laptop and tapped away at the keyboard. "Autumn 2010. It was my second year at the helm. Let's have a look." She scanned the screen in front of her. "There were twelve patients altogether from September until November. Four men and eight women."

"Could you make me a copy, please," Smith asked. "And I'll also need the names of everybody who has access to that information plus a list of all the people who were working here at that time."

Kelly tapped away at a few keys, stood up and left the room without explanation. She returned a few minutes later with two sheets of paper. "The names of the guests are here," she handed Smith one of the pages. "And the staff who worked here at the time are on this one. Please don't let me regret this. If it gets out that we're in the habit of divulging our guests' information, we'll go out of business."

"You have my word," Smith repeated. "Thank so much for your time." He stood up and stared at the woman in the photograph. "Who's that? That's an Arab isn't it?"

"I'm impressed. You know your horses. I hate the things to be honest. That's Fiona – she's my partner. Now, if you don't mind, I have a lot to do."
"We'll probably need to talk to you again."
"I'm not going anywhere."

Smith folded the papers and put them in his back pocket. He walked back down the corridor and stopped at the reception desk. The same man as before was sitting there talking on the phone. He ended the call and looked up at Smith.
"Will there be anything else? Would you like to make an appointment to find out about rehabilitation? I can email you the rates if you like."
"Maybe some other time."
Cheeky bastard.
"How long have you worked here?"
"Four years."
"And what do you think of Miss Bowen?"
"She's strict but fair – you have to be to make a go of a place like this. Some of the patients we get here are in desperate need of that kind of discipline."
Smith patted the papers in his back pocket. "Thanks, mate. I'll let you know if I change my mind about booking myself in."

Smith got in his car and took the papers from his pocket. He threw them on the passenger seat and started the engine. He reversed out of the parking spot and drove away from the rehabilitation centre. His phone started to ring. The screen told him it was Baldwin.
"What's up?" he said.
"There's been another one, Sarge," Baldwin said. "Another woman was found dead by her cleaning lady an hour ago."
"Hold on," Smith pulled over to the side of the road and opened up the list of ex-patients at the Weldon Centre. "Who is she?"
"She's had her throat slashed, Sarge."

"What's her name, Baldwin?" Smith scanned the list.

"Ashley White."

Smith gasped at the names on the list. Ashley White's name was there, but it was the name at the very bottom that made his heart feel like it was trying to escape from his chest – *Erica Whitton.*

CHAPTER THIRTY NINE

This has to be some kind of a mistake, Smith thought as he drove far too quickly through the city to the address Baldwin had given him, *Whitton would've never lied to me about spending time in rehab.*
He glanced over at the list again – there it was in black and white at the bottom of the piece of paper – *Erica Whitton.*
Eight women and four men. We can discard the men – that much has been made obvious, Ashley White is the fourth one so that leaves four more women. Including Whitton.

He pushed the thought aside and parked behind Yang Chu's Ford Focus. Baldwin was talking to DI Brownhill outside the house. Smith got out the car and walked up to them.

"Ashley White was on the list I got from the rehab centre," he said to Brownhill.

"How many names were actually on that list?" the DI asked.

"Eleven," Smith lied. "Four men and seven women."

"Then there's three women left," Baldwin said. "We have to find those women."

"Hold your horses," Brownhill warned. "What exactly do you propose to say to them? Sorry, but you're on some kind of hit-list. You'd better lay low for a while."

"We have to warn them, boss," Smith said. "Their lives are in danger."
As well as Whitton's.
Smith had a sudden urge to get home as quickly as possible. He couldn't bear being away from Whitton any longer. "Do you need me here, boss?" he asked the DI.

"You're the DS here, in case you've forgotten. We have a serial murderer on our hands and you have by far more experience than Bridge and Yang Chu. Is there somewhere else you'd rather be?"

"I just wanted to go home and check on Whitton. That thing with the giant in the garden has finally hit home – I need to check to see if she's alright. I'll be an hour, tops."

"I was there earlier," Brownhill said. "She's promised to keep the doors locked. Your presence is required here." She pointed to Ashley White's house. "It's not a pretty sight in there."

Smith tried not to think of Whitton and Laura as he stepped inside the house. Grant Webber was already there. He seemed to be taking a particular interest in something on the coffee table in the middle of the living room.

"Afternoon, Webber," Smith said. "What have you found?"

"Unworthy," Webber didn't look up. "It's been carved into the wood on the table."

"So it is the same killer then?"

"Definitely. What took you so long? The call came in over an hour ago."

"I had an appointment at an alcohol rehab centre."

"About bloody time."

"Very funny. Where's the woman?"

"Upstairs. She was in bed when she was killed by the looks of things – there's a lot of blood on the sheets and the mattress."

Smith walked up the stairs. Yang Chu was on his way down.

"How bad is it?" Smith asked him.

"Bad," Yang Chu replied. "But nowhere near as bad as the first one. Nice clean cut to the neck. She probably won't have felt a thing. What did you find out from the rehab place?"

"Not here. There's too many people around. We'll go over everything back at the station."

He carried on up the stairs and went in the main bedroom. Bridge was talking to one of Webber's forensics officers by the window.

"Sarge," Bridge nodded. "We've got another serial killer haven't we?"

"Looks like it."

"She had a four year old boy. He's staying over at a friend's house. At least he wasn't here when it happened."

Smith moved closer to the bed. The woman lying there appeared to be in her mid to late forties. Her hair was black but it was obviously dyed – the grey was coming through at the roots. She was lying on her back with her head on the pillow. The wound in her neck was deep.

"What do you think, Sarge?" Bridge asked.

"She was killed during the night or this morning – she's wearing her nightgown. She could have been asleep when it happened. Was there any sign of a break in?"

"Nothing yet," Webber's forensics officer replied. "We haven't quite finished but the initial search didn't reveal anything. No broken windows, buggered up doors. Nothing."

Smith had the urge to go home again.

This could've been Whitton, he thought. *It could've been Whitton next.*

He left the room, ran down the stairs two at a time and left the house. He walked past Baldwin and Brownhill and without saying a word he got in his car and sped off down the street. He screeched to a halt outside his house and jumped out the car. He didn't even bother to lock the doors. He turned the key in the lock on his front door and ran inside.

"Whitton! Where are you?"

No answer.

"Whitton!" Smith shouted again, louder this time.

He found her in the living room. She was lying on the sofa with Laura on her chest. They were both fast asleep. Smith walked over and placed his arms around both of them. Whitton opened her eyes but Laura didn't stir.
"What's going on?" Whitton said.
"Nothing," Smith didn't know what else to say. "I was in the area and I thought I'd come and check in with my girls."
He picked up his sleeping daughter and carried her upstairs. "I won't let anything bad happen to either of you." He placed her in the cot at the end of the bed and kissed her on the forehead.

"What's really going on?" Whitton asked Smith when he came back downstairs.
Smith told her about Ashley White. The word *Unworthy* had been carved into the coffee table.
"That's four now," Whitton said. "Do you think we'll ever catch this bastard?"
"I don't know." Smith didn't know how to bring up the topic of the Weldon rehab centre. "I paid a visit to Kirkham today."
Whitton's face was blank.
"The Weldon centre," Smith elaborated. "It's a rehabilitation facility."
Still not one spark of recognition.
"Never heard of it," Whitton said.
"The woman who runs the place gave me a list of everybody who was there at the same time as Julie Phelps, Magda Collins and Joy Williams. There were 12 names on the list. Four men and eight women. We can discard the men so that leaves eight. Four of those women have been killed."
"So there are four left. This is sick."
"Your name was on that list, Whitton. And I think that's why that ogre was here in our garden the other day. Your name is on that bloody list. Why didn't you tell me you'd spent some time in rehab? I thought we told each other everything? It's nothing to be ashamed of."

"Are you insane?" the expression on Whitton's face was something Smith had never seen before. It was one of utter disbelief. "Do you honestly think I'd lie about something like that?"

"Are you saying you weren't there the same time as those other women?"

"Are you even listening to yourself? Let me put it in a way you might understand. One – I've never set foot in a rehab centre and, two, if I had I wouldn't bullshit you about it. I think you'd better get back to work."

"But Whitton…"

"Just get out. I don't even know who you are sometimes. I thought we trusted each other."

"Of course we do. But your name was on the list."

"Please, just leave me alone."

She went upstairs without saying anything further.

Smith watched her go. His head was spinning.

What the hell is going on here?

His feet hadn't touched the ground since being woken up on Monday morning to be told about the brutal murder of Julie Phelps. He was about to go upstairs to talk to Whitton when his phone started to ring in his pocket.

"Smith," he answered it.

It was Yang Chu. "Sarge, the DI asked me to get hold of you. Webber found something peculiar at Ashley White's place."

"I'll be there in ten minutes."

"Brownhill's called an emergency briefing back at the station at four-thirty."

Smith looked at his watch. That was in thirty minutes. "I'll be there. What did Webber find?"

"Your guess is as good as mine. Brownhill's being rather cagy. She's been acting weird these past few days."

"I'll see you there," Smith said and rang off.

He debated whether to go upstairs and try and smooth things out with Whitton but he decided against it – he'd leave her to calm down a bit. He put his phone back in his pocket and left the house, making sure to lock the door behind him.

CHAPTER FORTY

The whole team was in the conference room when Smith went inside. Even DCI Chalmers was there.

"I got here as soon as I could," Smith said. "What's going on?"

"All in good time," Brownhill said. "How's Whitton?"

"As well as can be expected. Let's get started."

"Before we begin," Brownhill said. "There's a press conference scheduled for six-thirty this evening. I expect everybody in this room to attend. Hence the emergency briefing. Henry has gone over the material we have and he's outlined exactly how we are to approach the press conference."

Baldwin looked puzzled. "Henry?"

"Henry Short," Bridge explained. "The press liaison officer. He's quite a character."

"Anyway," Brownhill continued. "Let's press on. First things first – Smith, could you fill us in on what you found at the rehab centre?"

"Weldon rehabilitation centre," Smith said. "It's quite an upmarket place. Julie Phelps, Magda Collins and Joy Williams all spent time there in the autumn of 2010. As did Ashley White."

"That's that then," Bridge said. "That's definitely the connection. Four women dead – all of them were alkies in 2010."

"Thank you, detective," Brownhill said. "Smith, please continue."

"There were 12 people there at that time – four men and eight women."

"I thought you said there were 11," Baldwin said.

"Yes," Brownhill said. "I remember you mentioning 11 people."

"Listen up," Smith wasn't really sure how he was going to say the words that were formulating in his head. "This is all very bizarre but the last name on the list was Whitton's."

"Whitton spent time in rehab?" Yang Chu exclaimed.

"She denied it," Smith said. "I don't know what's going on but Whitton said she's never been to the place."

"And you didn't believe her?" Brownhill said.

"I don't know. All of this is messing with my head."

"How many Erica Whitton's can there be in York?" Bridge said.

Yang Chu looked at Smith. "That's why that giant was in your garden. Whitton's name was on the list. Oh my God."

"There has to be some kind of a mistake," Baldwin joined in. "If Whitton said she wasn't there, I believe her. I don't think I've ever met such an honest person before."

"Maybe she's embarrassed," Bridge suggested. "She's ashamed that she used to be an alkie."

"Bridge," Brownhill said. "That's enough. You're not helping here."

"Smith. " Chalmers had been listening intently. "Did you even bother to check with the centre if this Erica Whitton matches our Erica Whitton's description?"

Smith felt like an idiot. One phone call was all it would take to clear the matter up.

"Baldwin," he said. "I want you to get hold of Kelly Bowen at the rehab centre – ask her to email the details of the four remaining women on that list. This mystery Erica Whitton included."

"Right," Brownhill said while they waited for Baldwin. "Grant did a thorough job at Ashley White's house, as usual and he found something very odd."

"The suspense is killing us," Smith said and instantly regretted saying it. Brownhill ignored him. She opened up a laminated file. "Ashley White died as a result of loss of blood caused by a deep wound to her throat. We're still waiting on the time of death but the initial report would suggest she was killed sometime last night. The blood had congealed and rigor had started to set in. Ashley White lost a substantial amount of blood. The sheets and the mattress were soaked and that brings me to what forensics discovered. Grant found a hand print in the blood on the duvet cover."

Bridge sighed. "Is that it?"

"I'm not finished. All the evidence from the first three murders would suggest that a very large man was involved – the size 13 boot print, two witness reports…"

"Not to mention that giant that Whitton found in our back garden," Smith added.

"But the handprint on the bed was quite petite," Brownhill said.

"Maybe this giant has small hands," Yang Chu suggested.

"Donald Trump hands," Bridge added and started to laugh.

"Bridge," Brownhill said. "This is your last warning. This man does not have small hands – The bruises on Joy Williams' neck prove that his hands are much larger than average."

"What about the dead woman?" Smith pointed out. "She could have put her hand to her neck to stop the bleeding and made a handprint on the covers."

"Grant knows his job," Brownhill snorted. "This handprint was made by somebody else."

Baldwin rushed into the room.

"Well," Smith realised his heart was beating much faster than usual. "What have we got?"

"Of the remaining four women on the list," Baldwin said. "Only three are still alive. Miss Bowen heard that Beatrice Hall succumbed to cancer last year."

"What about this Erica Whitton?"

"Unless Whitton's lying about her age, it's not her. This Erica Whitton is a forty five year old mother of three who's now living in Harrogate."

"Shit," Smith said. "Shit, shit, shit."

"You've got some serious groveling to do," Chalmers said. "What the hell is wrong with you?"

"What about the other two women?" Smith said in an attempt to change the subject.

"Vanessa Quinn and Gloria Palmer. Miss Bowen didn't seem to know much about what had become of them."

"We need to find them," Smith said. "They're in danger."

Brownhill looked at Baldwin.

"I'll get onto it," Baldwin said and left the room again.

Smith stood up and headed for the door.

"Where do you think you're going?" Brownhill asked.

"To buy the biggest bunch of flowers I can find." He looked at Chalmers. "And then I've got some serious groveling to do."

"We've got a press conference in an hour," Brownhill reminded him.

"Me and the press don't exactly see eye to eye, boss." Smith said and left the room before Brownhill had a chance to argue.

* * *

Smith unlocked the door to his house, went inside and locked it again. Whitton was in the kitchen feeding Laura. Smith put the flowers he'd bought on the table and put his hands on Whitton's neck.

"Do you think a bunch of flowers and a shoulder rub is going to make everything alright?" Whitton brushed his hands away.

"I'm sorry," Smith said. "I don't know what I was thinking – I'm sorry."

"Rehab? Don't you think if I'd been in rehab I'd have told you?"

"I know – I'm an idiot."

"You can say that again."

"You have a namesake."

"I'd gathered that."

"She's forty five, she's got three kids and she lives in Harrogate."

Smith put his hands back on her shoulders and started to massage gently.
"I'm still mad at you. Don't think you can make it go away just like that. Rub a bit harder."
Smith pressed his fingers into the muscles of Whitton's shoulders. "There's a press conference about to start. I managed to get out of it."
"Probably for the best. You know how you can get with that lot."
"Are you hungry?"
"Starving. Are you actually going to cook something?"
"Of course not. It's still early – I was thinking of introducing Marge to this beautiful lady here. And grabbing a couple of Steak and Ale pies at the same time."
Laura finished her milk and belched. Theakston and Fred arrived on the scene and sat to attention. The Bull Terrier and the repulsive Pug had heard the words *Steak and Ale pie* and were instantly alert.
"We'll get you guys a takeaway," Smith promised. He looked at Whitton. "What do you say?"
"I still haven't forgiven you," Whitton said although she was finding it hard not to smile.

CHAPTER FORTY ONE

The Hog's head was quiet for a Friday evening. Smith was glad – he didn't want Laura's first experience of a pub to be one of loud noise and rowdy customers. He was carrying Laura's high chair. Whitton was holding on to the baby. Marge was leafing through some papers behind the bar. She looked up when she saw them approach and beamed from ear to ear.
"She's gorgeous," she was looked at Whitton. "She's lucky she inherited your looks and not his. Give her here."
Whitton passed Laura across the bar and Marge held on carefully. "You're going to cause your parents some serious problems when you get a bit older. All the boys are going to love you."
"Marge," Smith said. "She's six months old. Don't give me nightmares already."
"She weighs a ton," Marge said and handed Laura back to Whitton.
"She never stops eating," Whitton told her.
"Pint?" Marge asked Smith.
"Please, Marge. Make that two. And a couple of steak and ale pies. Could you organise another two for takeaway for the dogs?"
"Coming up."

Smith and Whitton sat at their usual table by the fireplace. Smith secured Laura into her high chair and went to the bar to fetch the drinks. "The press conference is about to begin," he said when he sat back down again. "I hope they don't let Bridge do any of the talking. The DI insisted that every one of us be there."
Whitton took a long sip of the beer. "Who do you think is going to get the DS job?"
"Your guess is as good as mine. Bridge is his own worst enemy. I think Yang Chu is ahead on points at the moment."

"I think I'd prefer to take orders from Bridge – Yang Chu can be a bit anal at times."

"I agree. Can we talk about something else?"

"Like what? Rehab?"

"I said I was sorry. You're not going to let me forget that, are you?"

Whitton finished what was left in her glass in one go. "Well if I was in rehab, it didn't work, did it. How about another pint? That one went down well."

"That's why I love you, Erica Whitton," Smith said. "I see you haven't lost your touch since the pregnancy."

"I'm Yorkshire through and through. And I'm thirsty."

Smith returned with two more beers. Laura was glugging away at a bottle of milk.

"So you do love me?" Whitton said.

"Of course I do – I don't say it enough."

Whitton took a long slurp from the glass. It had been a while since she'd had anything to drink and the beer was already making her feel quite tipsy.

"Why don't we get married?"

Smith was so taken aback that he almost choked on the beer in his mouth.

"Did I just hear correctly?"

"Why not? We've been together for quite a while – we have a child together, why not get married?"

"I thought it was the bloke's job to ask the woman."

"This is the twenty-first century. What do you think?"

"OK, let's do it. Erica Smith – it has a certain ring to it."

"Who said I wanted to take your name as well?"

Marge arrived at the table and placed two steak and ale pies in front of them. "The takeaways are behind the bar. The dogs don't mind it if they're cold, do they?"

"They won't even notice," Smith said. "Thanks Marge. I'm getting married."

Whitton slapped him on the shoulder.

"It must be the beer," Smith carried on. "Erica had just asked me to marry her."

"It must be the beer," Marge agreed. "I suppose she could do a lot worse. I'd better get back to the bar – the place is starting to fill up."

She walked off shaking her head.

"Why did you tell her that?" Whitton asked.

"I didn't realise it was a secret."

"You've got a lot to learn."

"When were you planning on doing this thing?" Smith asked.

"As soon as possible. We can have an Autumn wedding. There's still a lot to organise."

"That's your department. Eat up – these pies are getting cold."

"How's the fulsome Bryony Brownhill?" Smith asked as they ate their food. "You and her are becoming quite close friends."

"No we're not," Whitton protested. "She's was just concerned. I still think it's quite sweet in a way."

"Don't let her fool you – even without the moustache and a bit of makeup she's still an ogre."

"She's a woman who needs the same things as any other woman. She's had quite a tragic life."

"You mean the relationship with Webber?"

Whitton cut up a piece of pie and added some mashed potato on the fork.

"She told me some things I don't think she's spoken to anybody else about."

"What things?"

"She can't have kids," Whitton put the fork in her mouth.

"Probably for the best."

"And she had a brother who died."

"That's life, Erica. We've all had shit in our lives. I've lost pretty much everything – you should know that."

"There was something else," Whitton said. "It was something in the way she poured it all out to me. It was like she wanted to confess."

"Confess?" Smith took a long swig of beer. "Confess to what?"

"I don't know. She showed me a photo that was taken before her brother died. It was quite weird, actually."

"Weird?"

"I don't know," Whitton said once more. "I just got the feeling she wasn't there to find out how I was – she wanted another woman to understand what she'd been through."

Smith lay his knife and fork down. "Bollocks. What was in this photo?"

"It was a photo of her brother before he died. He was so young."

"What did he die of?"

"Meningitis. He was a huge kid – bigger than any kid I've seen before, but he was weak."

Smith finished what was left on his plate and took a sip of his beer. "You need to get back to work. You're going soft in your old age."

* * *

Back at the station the press conference was about to get underway. Brownhill, Bridge, Yang Chu and Baldwin were standing at the front of the conference room talking to Henry Short, the press liaison officer. The room was slowly filling up with journalists – news of the four dead women had spread and the press were eager for answers.

"Do you think you're ready for this?" Henry asked Bridge. "It's quite daunting out there.

"I have done this before," Bridge told him. "During the Jimmy Fulton thing, remember."

"I could've headed it up," Yang Chu argued. "I'm perfectly capable of talking to the press. You'll probably say something stupid."

"You can do the next one," Bridge offered. "It's all been set up. I can handle it."

"Then I suppose you're ready," Henry sighed. "I'll lead off and then the floor's yours. We've got quite a turnout this evening. Does anybody know if Superintendant Smyth will be joining us?"

"I hope not," Brownhill replied. "It's better without him."

"Very well – let's get started."

Bridge followed him to the long table at the front. Brownhill and Baldwin sat on either side of him. Yang Chu stayed standing where he was.

Henry Short turned on the microphone. "Good evening ladies and gentlemen and thank you all for coming at such short notice. Detective constable Bridge will be heading up the conference and he will answer any questions you have at the end. DC Bridge."

"Thank you, Henry," Bridge looked at the crowd of people waiting to hear what he was about to say. "And thank you for coming. As you're all probably aware, four women have been killed in the past week."

A red-haired woman stood up. "Four? I thought there were three."

Henry Short leaned into the microphone. "Please, Susan – Any questions will be answered at the end."

The woman sat back down.

"Four women have been murdered," Bridge continued. "We have reason to believe their murderer is the same man. We have a witness who got a look at this man and we have obtained a very good description of him. We have a photo-fit and you will all have access to it in due course. Some new information has come to light and we have every confidence that he will be apprehended very soon." He looked across at Henry Short. Henry nodded. "Are there any questions?"

The red haired woman stood up again. "Do you have the names of these four women?"

"For the time being their names will kept out of it," Bridge said. "For the sake of their poor families."

"How were they killed?" a man in his late fifties asked. "Gary Powers – York Evening Post."

"They were all killed in different ways," Bridge said. "We have no reason to believe the MO's are relevant."

"Not relevant?" Powers scoffed. "OK, do you have anything else to give us? You say you reckon one man killed these four women – why do you think that? Is there a connection between these women?"

Bridge's head was spinning. "We believe there is but I'm not at liberty to divulge anything further until we've checked all the facts."

"So you don't actually have much then, do you?" Powers said and sat down.

A timid looking man with a very long face stood up. "This witness you've got - the one who got a look at this bloke. Who is it?"

"She was the babysitter for one of the victims. She was there when he carried out the murder."

"When was this?"

"The woman was killed on Tuesday.

"And you've had a description of him since then and you've done nothing about it."

Bridge wanted to floor to swallow him up. He didn't know what to say.

"Detective," the man urged.

"The woman who saw our killer was traumatised," Bridge said. "We only got the photo-fit from her much later."

"But you've still been hanging on to it? Surely, if this maniac's face was put out there straight away, someone may have recognised him and he'd be in custody by now."

The man clearly wasn't as meek and mild as his appearance suggested. Bridge realised he was starting to sweat. "Like I said, you will all have access to that photo-fit. Anything else?"

A very tall woman stood up. "Where's DS Smith this evening? It's not like him to miss a press conference."

"DS Smith had other pressing matters to attend to," was all Bridge could think of to say.

"DC Bridge," the woman said. "All you've given us is a photo-fit of the man you suspect is behind these killings. Four women are dead – do we have a serial killer out there somewhere? Should the women of York be afraid?"

Bridge was afraid of this. "Absolutely not. We have it on good authority that this man is working to a pattern – he is not killing indiscriminately. There is no need for panic to set in."

"What pattern is he working to?" the woman wasn't giving up.

"I said before and I'll say it again, I'm not at liberty to disclose that until we've conducted further enquiries into the matter."

"Poppycock," an elderly man said without bothering to stand up. "Ken Swales – Herald. You lot know something and you're holding back. You've kept the killer's description to yourself – what other information are you withholding? In all my forty years in this game, I've never heard such twaddle in my life. If you've got nowt, tell us you've got nowt – don't blab on about your 'we have reason to believe' and your 'we are not at liberty to discuss' tosh. I'm sick and tired of it."

The room fell silent. Henry Short stepped in.

"If that's everything, we'll finish up there. The photo-fit of the suspect will be available to all of you shortly. Thank you all for coming."

He switched off the microphone before anybody could ask any further questions.

CHAPTER FORTY TWO

"That was a nightmare," Bridge said in the canteen ten minutes later. "I'm not doing that again in a hurry."

"I could've done a much better job," Yang Chu bragged. "You came across as a tad incompetent in there."

"You try facing that many people and thinking on your feet. You'd have probably made a right balls-up of it."

"You two," Brownhill said. "Stop your bickering. It's done now. That lot are never satisfied."

"What now then?" Baldwin asked.

Brownhill glanced at the clock on the wall. "It's late – the man's description will be in all the papers tomorrow, let's see what comes of it."

"Are you going to Whitton's barbecue tomorrow?" Bridge asked the DI.

"I've been thinking about that and, for once I'm inclined to agree with Smith – it could be just what we all need."

"But what about the investigation?" Yang Chu argued. "How can we go to a party while this man is still out there? What about the other two women on that list? Vanessa Quinn and Gloria Palmer still live in York. We need to warn them. They could be in danger."

"We're all starting to show signs of cracking," Brownhill said. "Plodding on is only going to make it worse. I'd say a day off is what we all need right now."

"I agree," Chalmers was standing in the doorway.

Nobody had heard him arrive. He'd been listening in to the whole conversation.

"Banging your heads against a brick wall for too long only cracks heads. You need some time to step back and repair your brains. Besides, it's a free feed and I for one am not going to turn that down."

* * *

"I'm stuffed," Whitton leaned back in her chair and sighed. "That was the best steak and ale pie I've ever had. I don't think I'll be able to eat for a week after that."

"Don't forget the barbecue tomorrow," Smith reminded her. "I'm planning a feast. You don't have a birthday every day. How old are going to be, again?"

"Younger than you'll ever be. I need the loo."

Smith watched her go. The pub was busy now – young couples were sitting at tables discussing where they were going to move onto next, elderly men were nursing half-pints of ale at the bar. Smith didn't spot the thirty-something woman with the long dark hair sitting alone at the furthest table from the bar. If he'd seen her, he would have noticed she'd been taking a keen interest in their table since they'd arrived in the pub. Whitton walked straight past the woman's table without paying her any attention. The woman stood up and headed for the door.

She walked away from the Hog's Head and turned right onto London Road. She carried on for a further two hundred metres and stopped outside number 16. The lights were on inside the house. The road was deserted – the woman hadn't seen a single person the whole way. She walked up the path and knocked on the door. It was opened a short while later by a blonde woman in her late twenties.

"Vanessa Quinn?" the woman said.

"That's right. Is everything alright?"

She took out the fake police ID. "DS Brown. Can I come in? I'm afraid I have some bad news."

"What is it? Is it Gregg? Is it Sean? Has something happened to my baby?"

"Please, Mrs Quinn, it would be better if we talked inside."

"What's this all about?" Vanessa asked in the living room. "Please tell me what's going on. If it isn't Gregg or Sean, what is it?"

"Is Gregg your husband?"

"We're separated. He has Sean every second weekend. What the hell is going on?"

"I need to ask you some questions first."

"What questions?"

"Do you mind if I use your bathroom?"

"Just tell me what you're here for."

The woman stood up, took something out of her pocket and stuck it into Vanessa Quinn's leg. Vanessa gasped – a syringe was sticking out of her thigh. Her vision started to blur and a wave of numbness spread through her whole body. She tried to speak but the words wouldn't come.

"Do you mind if I use your bathroom?" the woman asked again but Vanessa could no longer hear her.

When she woke, Vanessa Quinn had no idea where she was. Her head was pounding and her mouth felt incredibly dry. She opened her eyes wider and flinched at the bright light. She tried to move her arms but it was impossible – they wouldn't budge. She realised she was lying on her back – the oppressive light that was blinding her eyes was a ceiling lamp – her ceiling lamp. She couldn't move her legs either. She felt as though she was paralysed.

"Welcome back, sleepy head," a familiar voice said from somewhere in the room.

Vanessa suddenly remembered what had happened earlier.

The police woman, the syringe.

She tried to talk but her lips were too dry. She ran her tongue over them but the saliva in her mouth appeared to have dried out.

"Don't try and talk just yet," the woman told her. "Right now, I want you to listen instead. Do you think you can do that?"

"Who are you?" Vanessa managed.

She didn't see the hand as it rushed through the air and slapped her on the side of the face. She felt a stinging sensation and her cheek started to burn. "If I have to, I'll tape your mouth shut too. I told you I want you to listen. Now, do you think you can do that?"

Vanessa managed to nod.

"Good. I'll try to keep this brief."

She took off her glasses and removed the long wig. Vanessa gasped.

"You? It can't be."

"Not everything is as it seems, Vanessa."

The woman left the room and returned a few seconds later. Vanessa saw she had something in her hands – a laptop computer. She booted it up and pressed a few keys.

"I want to you look at something." She brought up a Facebook page. "You really ought to change your privacy settings – letting people into your life online can be dangerous, deadly even."

She put the screen in front of Vanessa's face. It took a while for her eyes to focus but after a few seconds she knew exactly what she was looking at – it was her own profile page. There in front of her were her list of friends, her photographs, everything.

"There's Julie," the woman scrolled down. "And Magda, and Joy and, oh look – that looks like Ashley doesn't it? All with their cosy little lives for the whole world to see."

Vanessa forced herself to look at the photographs. After their time in the rehabilitation centre these women had become close – they shared a bond that very few people would understand. They'd remained friends even after all of them had left Weldon. They'd been supportive in the tough times and they'd shared the happy times with each other. It was these *happy times* that filled the screen in front of Vanessa's face – photographs of the women with their children, holiday snaps, birthday parties.

"You're all unworthy," the woman screamed so loud that it made Vanessa's ears ring. "Unworthy!"

The woman raised the laptop in the air and brought it down with all her strength on the coffee table in the middle of the room. The screen shattered and pieces of metal covered the floor.

"What do you want?" Vanessa asked her.

She watched in horror as the woman picked up one of the larger shards of metal from the laptop and moved closer.

"Unworthy," she said in a voice not much more than a whisper.

She looked at the jagged piece of metal in her hand and sliced open Vanessa's throat.

CHAPTER FORTY THREE

"Do you think you've got enough meat there?" Whitton pointed to the stack of steaks, sausages and chops on the kitchen table.
"Do you think I should have bought some more?" Smith asked.
"I was being sarcastic. There's enough there to feed an army."
"We are feeding an army. The York Police force army. Besides, these two won't let any of it go to waste."
Theakston and Fred had been taking a keen interest in the meat for the barbecue ever since Smith had returned from the shops. The Bull Terrier and the hideous Pug hadn't let it out of their sight since Smith had come through the door.
"What time did you tell everyone to get here?" Whitton asked.
"Around two. It'll give me time to crank up the fire and get it hot enough to cook on."
"Just try not to burn it."
"I am Australian in case you've forgotten. Barbies come natural to us."
"You've been here too long – you've almost turned into a Yorkshireman."
"Did you mean what you said last night?" Smith changed the subject. "About us getting married?"
"I only had two pints – of course I remember. Why, are you having second thoughts?"
"Of course not. I'm starting to get used to the idea. Mr and Mrs Smith."
"That part can't be helped. Anyway, I'm thinking of maybe keeping my maiden name."

Their conversation was cut short by a disturbance on the kitchen table. Theakston had managed to get up with the help of one of the chairs and was now making a beeline for the pile of raw meat.
"Bad dog," Whitton said.

Smith lifted him off the table and frog-marched him outside to the back garden. "You stay out there."

"That dog needs training," Whitton said.

"He's past training. Are we going to tell people about the wedding?"

"Of course. That's the general idea."

"I thought we could tell them all at the barbecue. Everyone will be here."

"If you like. I still can't believe Brownhill has agreed to give everyone time off during a murder investigation – she must be going soft in her old age."

"Chalmers agreed with her. It'll take our minds off things for a while."

Their guests started to arrive a couple of hours later. Chalmers was the first to come through the door. He was holding a bottle of scotch in his hand.

"Afternoon, boss," Smith said. "Long time no see. I'll get you a glass for that."

Bridge, Yang Chu and Baldwin all arrived at the same time a few minutes later. Bridge had brought two cases of lager with him.

"If you're going to do something," he said. "You might as well do it right. I'll pop a few in the fridge. Where's Brownhill?"

"Her and Webber aren't here yet," Smith said. "Go out to the garden. The fire's almost ready for the meat to go on."

Smith had put some chairs outside for everybody to sit on. They'd been lucky with the weather – the rain that had threatened to linger a couple of days earlier was showing no sign of returning. Smith carried the pile of meat outside and placed it on a small table.

"We've got rump steak, T bone, lamb and pork chops and a whole load of sausages for those of you who are less adventurous."

"I'll stick some music on," Whitton offered and walked back to the kitchen. A few seconds later, the intro to The Beatles' 'Back in the USSR' could be heard from inside the house.

"Good choice," Smith put his arms on her waist when she came back outside. "Shall we tell them now?"

Whitton shook her head. "Not yet. Brownhill and Webber aren't even here yet. Did you tell them the right time?"

"Of course I did. The DI needs a bit longer to do her makeup, remember. Maybe she needed a shave."

"You're terrible."

Right on cue, Brownhill and Webber appeared in the garden. Smith hoped that they hadn't been close enough to hear what he and Whitton were saying.

"Sorry we're a bit late," Brownhill said. "Grant had a flat tyre."

"Well, you're here now," Chalmers said. "Grab a drink. Bridge brought enough lager to sink a battleship. Sup up."

Smith turned the meat on the grill and smiled. The sun was beating down, the smell of slowly cooking steaks and chops filled the air and, not once had anybody mentioned the investigation that had taken over their lives in the past week.

"Here's to York's finest," Chalmers raised a full glass of scotch in the air and spilled half of it in the process. "I don't give a monkey's arse what anybody says, this is the best police force in the country."

"How much has he had?" Whitton whispered to Smith.

"Not nearly as much as he's about to have. Let him enjoy himself. I'd drink like that too if I had to spend most of my working life with an idiot like old Smyth. We'll tell them after we've eaten, OK?"

"Alright," Whitton laughed and went to speak to Baldwin.

"Are you OK?" she asked.

Baldwin hadn't spoken much since she got there.

"Can I get you something to drink?" Whitton offered. "You don't have one."

"I don't drink that much. I'll grab one of Bridge's lagers in a minute. This is lovely. Do you know, it's only the second time I've ever been to a barbecue."
"Don't speak too soon. Smith's been away from Oz for so long, I'm not sure he even knows how to do it anymore."
Baldwin went inside the house. "I'll get that drink."
"I'd like to make another toast," Charmers' voice was getting louder and louder. "To Smith and Whitton and that little girl of theirs. Where is the little tyke, anyway?"
"She's asleep upstairs, boss," Smith said. "Luckily, she can sleep through anything."
"Well I'll drink to you three anyway." Chalmers patted Smith on the shoulder. "When's Whitton going to make an honest man of you?"
Smith looked over at Whitton. She rolled her eyes, smiled and shrugged.
"He's been dying to tell you all," she said. "We're getting married."
"Don't do it," Bridge screamed and downed what was left in his can.
Yang Chu came over and patted Smith on the back. "Congratulations, Sarge."
"Yes," Webber joined in. "Well done. I wish you all the best."
Even Brownhill had a smile on her face. Baldwin came out with a can of lager. She hadn't heard Smith's announcement and was curious as to what was going on.
"Did I miss something?"
"Smith and Whitton are getting married," Bridge told her. "Poor bastards."
"That's great news," Baldwin still looked stunned. "Congratulations."
She hugged Smith and Whitton in turn.

"Something's burning," Chalmers said. "I thought you knew how to cook on one of those things."
"It's not burning, boss," Smith said. "That's just the fat crisping up. It's how it's supposed to be."

"Well it smells burnt to me," Chalmers said. "But then again, half a bottle of scotch tends to numb the senses a bit."

Smith lit a cigarette. "Five more minutes and the food will be done. We've got some ready-made salads, potatoes and bread too."

He turned the meat one last time and took a swig of beer. He spotted his neighbour in the garden next door. "Would you care to join us?"

"Definitely not," the man scowled. "And I'd appreciate it if you kept the noise down – I've got the grand kids for the weekend and your racket is keeping them awake. It's time for their afternoon nap."

"I've got a six month old upstairs snoring her head off," Smith told him. "Are you sure you don't want to chuck a chop on the fire – it's still got plenty of heat left in it."

The neighbour walked off in disgust.

Arsehole, Smith thought and returned to the barbecue.

They ate in silence. Everybody except Baldwin tucked in with obvious gusto. Baldwin hardly ate at all – a sausage and a small salad was all she put on her plate. Chalmers managed to get through two steaks, one pork chop, one lamb chop and half a plateful of sausages.

"When was the last time you ate, boss?" Smith remarked when the plate was empty.

"Mrs Chalmers has put me on a strict diet," Chalmers said, licking his lips. "That was the best food I've had all year."

"Thanks," Smith said as his phone started to ring in the kitchen.

He ignored it – everyone who normally phoned him was sitting in his front garden. The ringing stopped and another mobile phone ringtone could be heard nearby. It was Grant Webber's. The head of forensics took out the phone, frowned and answered it. Smith watched as Webber listened intently to whoever was on the other end.

Webber put the phone back in his pocket. "It looks like the party's over. A fisherman has found a body in the river."

"Can't somebody else deal with it?" Bridge asked. "We're not the only coppers in York."

Webber looked at Smith with a grave expression on his face. "I think it would be better if we dealt with this one – the description of the man in the river matches the description Joy Williams' babysitter gave of the man who killed Mrs Williams. It looks like our Unworthy killer is no more."

CHAPTER FORTY FOUR

Smith drove with Baldwin to the spot where the fisherman had discovered the body in the river. Baldwin was very quiet.

"Is something wrong?" Smith asked her.

"Apart from being dragged away from a barbecue to see a body that's just been pulled out of the river?"

"You were acting strange at my place – you hardly said two words and you ate like a bird."

"It's nothing," Baldwin said. "Do you think this is our Unworthy killer?"

"Part of me hopes it is. But something doesn't feel right."

"That Smith gut-feeling again?"

"Something like that. It's too easy. Surely you don't believe the man we've been looking for all week would just be handed on a plate to us?"

"Maybe he developed a conscience," Baldwin suggested. "His guilt overcame him and he couldn't handle it anymore."

"Suicide?"

"Why not?"

Smith took the turn-off towards the river and slowed down. "No, something isn't right here."

Two police cars and an ambulance showed Smith the spot where the man had been found. A fire engine was also parked a short distance away. Smith parked next to one of the police cars and got out. He walked over to a uniformed officer he vaguely recognised.

"Walker, isn't it? What have we got?"

"Big guy, sir," PC Walker said. "That's what the fire department are doing here – they had to get him out with some kind of crane."

"Where's the body?"

"Under a sheet not far from where the old angler spotted him. Poor bastard – what a way to go."

"Thanks, Walker. I want you and the other uniform to keep the area clear. Webber's on his way – he won't appreciate anybody contaminating his crime scene."

"Can I say something, sir?"

"Make it quick."

"I'm not a detective but even I can see there won't be much of a crime scene. If he's been in the river a while, surely all the evidence will be long gone."

"Like you said, you're not a detective. You'd be amazed what forensics can do these days."

Webber arrived with Brownhill a few minutes later. They walked over to Baldwin who was standing next to the sheet that hid the mystery man in the river.

"Where's Smith?" Brownhill asked.

"Talking to the man who found the body, ma'am," Baldwin replied.

"Have you had a look?"

"I didn't think it was my place."

"Quite right," Webber agreed. "I'll take it from here."

Baldwin was relieved. The last thing she wanted to do was look at the dead body of a man found in the river. She walked away before Webber changed his mind.

The fisherman who found the body was talking to Smith on a park bench fifty metres away. He was in his late sixties and he had a weather-beaten face – he obviously spent a lot of time outdoors.

"Mr Hume," Smith said. "What time did you discover the man?"

"Call me Sid. It was five minutes before I phoned you lot. I've been instructed by the missus to keep my phone close. She likes to know where I am at all times. I've been mislaid in the past, you see."

Mislaid? Smith thought but decided not to press further.

"How did you happen to spot it?"

"You couldn't miss it. My eyes are worse than a rhino with cataracts but even I saw it. There's a natural dam that's built up over time from the twigs and other crap in the river – the rainfall we had the other day will have dumped more debris in there. It's right by where the fire engine is parked. I'll tell you a secret but you must promise to keep it to yourself."

"Of course."

"The fish like to congregate by this dam, you see. None of the other anglers seem to know about it and I don't let on but that's where I fish mostly."

"And that's where you saw the man?"

"I thought it was just some bin bags at first – some idiot had dumped the stuff in the river but bin bags don't have a bloody great bloated face attached to them, do they?"

"No they don't. How often have you been fishing down here?"

"Nigh on forty years. It was much better in the old days, I can tell you that. Before all these fancy apartments sprang up."

"Thank you, Sid. You've been very helpful."

Smith saw that Webber was still busy examining the body. He took out a cigarette and lit it. He walked down the walkway that ran along the river and stopped by the fire engine. He spotted the natural dam straight away. The current was being diverted by the sticks, grasses and other vegetation that had formed a natural structure under the water. He realised that what PC Walker had said was partly true. They would find nothing at the scene where the body was found – their only hope lay in what the body itself told them.

Smith threw his cigarette butt into the river and went over to Webber.

"What have we got?"

"I reckon this is our guy," Webber said. "Have a look for yourself."

Smith pulled back the sheet and gasped. A huge man was lying there. His facial features had been slightly bloated from the water but he did bear a striking resemblance to the photofit picture Joy Williams' babysitter had come up with.

"See what I mean," Webber added.

Smith was inclined to agree. "OK, let's say this is our guy – how did he end up here and why?"

"The path guys will give us TOD and exactly what happened. Why he ended up here is your department isn't it?"

"Baldwin thinks he may have developed a conscious and jumped."

"What do you think?"

"I think that's a bit too convenient. And I've yet to come across a serial killer with a conscience."

Smith took another look at the man lying there. His Yogi Bear face seemed almost peaceful with its doe eyes and droopy mouth.

Maybe Baldwin's right, he thought, *maybe he did decide enough was enough and ended it all.*

Two paramedics arrived and joined the two who were already on the scene. "They needed some help," the taller of the two said to Smith and looked at the body. "And I can see why. This guy must weigh about twenty five stone."

"I just hope he doesn't wreck the stretcher," the other man added.

They removed the sheet and lay it to one side. "Let's turn him over," the first paramedic suggested. "Lay him on the sheet and then we can take a corner each."

Two of the men took the feet and the other two took hold of his hands. "On three," the tall paramedic said. "One, two, three."

They managed to roll him onto his stomach without incident.

"Now," the tall paramedic instructed. "Take a corner each and lift him onto the stretcher."

"Hold on," Grant Webber moved closer. He'd obviously spotted something. "Look at the back of his neck."

"What is it?" Smith asked.

"The path guys will confirm it but that mark on his neck looks like a knife wound." He gazed up at Smith. "It looks like you were right – he didn't suddenly develop a conscience and jump into the river, somebody gave him a bit of help."

CHAPTER FORTY FIVE

Smith parked outside the hospital and stopped the engine. He'd followed the ambulance transporting the mystery giant's body to the mortuary.
"Are you sure you want to do this?" he asked Baldwin. "Have you attended autopsies before?"
"No," Baldwin admitted. "But there always has to be a first one, doesn't there?"
Smith was impressed. He remembered his first autopsy. He'd been concentrating so hard on trying not to pass out that, still to this day he can't remember anything of what went on in that room that day. They went inside and Baldwin followed Smith along the corridor towards the mortuary. They stopped in front of a small reception desk.
"Afternoon," Smith said to a pimply youth behind the desk. "Do you know where they took the man they found in the river?"
"Room 3," the youth told him. "Apparently they flagged it as urgent. Who are you?"
Smith took out his ID. "DS Smith and this is PC Baldwin. Who's in charge of the autopsy?"
"Dr Dessai."
Smith had never met him before. Since his close friend Paul 'The Ghoul' Johnson had been killed the mortuary hadn't been the same. The Ghoul had somehow managed to make death a lot more lighthearted than it ought to be – entertaining even.
"Where is he now?" he asked. "This Dr Dessai?"
"She. Dr Dessai is a woman. She'll be in her office. Is she expecting you?"
"Not exactly. We'll find her."
He set off down the corridor without further explanation.

They stopped outside a room with a brown door. Smith remembered the room well – it used to be The Ghoul's office. A brass plaque with 'Dr Dessai' on it was pinned to the door. Smith knocked on it.

"Come in," a deep, husky voice was heard from inside.

They went in. A petite woman was sitting behind a desk in front of a laptop computer. She looked up at Smith and Baldwin and smiled.

"That was quick. Detective sergeant Smith, I assume?"

"That's right," Smith said. "And this is PC Baldwin."

Dr Dessai held out a hand. "Pleased to meet you. I've been informed that this is an emergency. Time is of the essence as it were. Have you been drinking?"

"I was having a barbecue for my girlfriend's birthday," Smith said. "I had a few beers."

"I suppose a few beers isn't going to make a difference. I know the feeling – always on duty. You knew Paul, didn't you?"

"Very well. He was a bit on the odd side but he was a good man."

"Cutting up dead people, it helps if you're a bit on the odd side. I hardly knew Paul Johnson but he had quite a reputation. Shall we get to it then?" She stood up and looked at Baldwin. "You're not squeamish are you?"

"I don't think so," Baldwin said.

"Let's go and find out."

The huge man the fisherman had found in the river had been placed on his stomach on the metal table in one of the autopsy rooms. Smith shivered. The room was at least fifteen degrees colder than the rest of the hospital. Dr Dessai washed her hands in the sink against the wall.

"Let's get started, shall we?"

Smith moved closer to the table. Baldwin observed from a few metres away. Dr Dessai lay a selection of surgical instruments on a small tray adjacent to the table. "Is this the man in the papers this morning?"

"We have reason to believe he is," Smith said. "We'll have to compare the prints from the boots he was wearing and we'll need a cast of his hands to confirm it but I'm 99% certain this is our guy."

"Mr Webber said something similar."

"It's not often me and Webber are on the same page."

"Excuse me?"

"Nothing. Can you tell roughly the time of death?"

"All in good time." She put her hand to the mark on the man's neck. "This is interesting. I'd say this is a knife wound. Let's have a look shall we?"

Smith watched as she photographed the neck then, with a small file-like instrument, opened the entrance to the wound. She then proceeded to determine the depth of the incision with another mystery surgical instrument.

"We need to turn him over," she said. "I think we might need some help. He was weighed when he came in and he topped the scales at just under thirty stone. Wait here."

She left the room and returned with two orderlies.

"His head and torso weigh more than his legs," she informed them. "You two take a hand each and the detective and I will take the feet." She turned to look at Baldwin. "Are you OK? You look a bit pale."

"I'm fine," Baldwin insisted. "Can I help?"

"That won't be necessary. Let's do this."

The corpse was laid on his back without incident. The two orderlies left the room and Dr Dessai continued. "I'm going to begin by opening up his neck."

She made a cross incision in the throat and pulled back the skin. "The tip of the blade struck his trachea." She measured the distance from the back of his neck to where the knife blade struck. "15 centimetres. He's a big man with a bull neck – in an average person, the knife would have come out the other side."

"What does that tell us?" Baldwin was suddenly interested.

"Patience. You don't have to watch this part."

Baldwin did watch. She watched as Dr Dessai made a Y-shaped incision from each shoulder blade down to the middle of the stomach. She carefully pulled back the skin to expose the ribcage.

"Still with us?" she addressed both Smith and Baldwin.

"Are you going to find out if he was already dead before he ended up in the river?" Baldwin asked.

"Very good." Dr Dessai said as she removed the entire ribcage, followed by the larynx, oesophagus and ligaments. The organs were lifted out carefully.

"I'm going to need to do a full examination," Dr Dessai told them, "but for the sake of your curiosity, I can give you a slight head's-up."

She placed the lungs on a separate table and took out a smaller, much sharper-looking scalpel. "There you have it." She sliced open the organ. "If he drowned, there would be water in his lungs. This man's heart stopped beating before he hit the water. It appears that the knife severed his windpipe, he drew a last breath or two and that was it."

"Something doesn't make sense," Smith found himself thinking out loud again.

"Go on," Dr Dessai urged.

"It'll come to me later. Thank you for helping us out at such short notice. The Ghoul would've liked you."

CHAPTER FORTY SIX

"Are you OK?" Smith asked Baldwin as they made their way to his car.
"I'm fine. What was that about back there? The bit about something not making sense?"
"I was trying to fathom how someone could kill a man that size, transport him to the river and dump him. It would take at least three or four people to even carry him."
He opened the car and they both got in.
"It is odd," Baldwin agreed as Smith drove out of the hospital car park. "It took four of you just to turn him over. Where are we going?"
"To forensics. If I know Webber, he'll be busy comparing the boot print and the bruises found on Joy Williams' neck."

Smith's feeling turned out to be spot-on. Webber was analysing the bruise marks found on Joy Williams' neck when Smith and Baldwin walked in his lab at the new forensics building. Even though the building was now a few years old it was still known as the new forensics building. Nobody seemed to know where the budget for such a modern, hi-tech department had come from when most other departments were suffering cut-backs – some speculated it wasn't totally above-board but whatever underhand dealings had gone on, the new forensics building was there to stay.
"Webber," Smith announced their presence. "I thought I might find you here. What have you got?"
Webber didn't look up from the computer screen he was studying. "The boot print found in Magda Collins' kitchen matches the boots the giant was wearing."
"Are you sure?" Baldwin asked.

"Positive. The ridges in the soles of footwear become unique as soon as the wearer puts them on. It's the same man. And just to make sure. Come and have a look at this."

Smith and Baldwin both looked at the computer screen.

"What are we supposed to be looking at?" Baldwin asked.

"This is a computer generated image of the dead man's hands," Webber pointed out. "From all directions." He tapped a few keys on the keyboard. "If we rotate them like this…"

"We get a view of them coming towards us," Smith said.

"As if he were about to put them around our necks," Baldwin cottoned on.

"Exactly," Webber brought up another image on the other side of the screen. "And this is a detailed analysis of the bruise marks on Joy Williams' throat. If we put them together we get this…"

"It's a perfect match," Smith exclaimed. "So our man in the river is definitely responsible for the murders of at least two of the women. What about Julie Phelps and the latest one, Ashley White?"

"That's going to take some more time," Webber said. "We'll need to go through everything we found at the crime scenes again but at least we have something to go on now – we have this man's fingerprints as well as samples of his DNA."

"It has to be the same man," Baldwin said. "You're forgetting the Unworthy part. It has to be the same man."

"I agree," Smith said. "But Webber still needs to confirm it. How much time are we talking about here?"

"It'll be a whole lot quicker if I'm left in peace," Webber said gruffly.

"Hint taken. Come on, Baldwin, there's someone we need to speak to."

* * *

Jessica Blakemore sat on the floor in her room at the Lemonwood hospital. Her eyes were closed and her arms were outstretched with her palms facing upwards. She was breathing in through her nose and out through her mouth.

"Shh," Smith said to Baldwin in the doorway.

Jessica opened her eyes. "You should try this," she looked directly at Smith. "It helps you to think straight. What do you want?"

"There's been a development," Smith told her. "Can we talk outside? I'm dying for a cigarette."

The clouds overhead promised more rain – thick cloaks of dark grey were smothering the white wisps that had lingered all day. Smith, Baldwin and Jessica chose a bench and sat down. Smith lit a cigarette and savoured the first rush of the nicotine.

"What's this development?" Jessica came right out with it.

"We've found the man responsible for killing all these women," Smith told her. "The Unworthy killer."

"That's quite a development. But surely you could have told me this over the phone. There's more isn't there."

"No," Smith lied. "There isn't. I just wanted to let you know in person. A fisherman found his body earlier today in the River Ouse."

"He's dead?"

"That's not all," Baldwin said. "He'd been stabbed in the back of the neck. He was dead before he hit the water."

"What do you want from me, Jason?" Jessica asked.

"I want to keep you in the loop," Smith said. "And to let you know you're losing your touch."

Jessica stood up. "Please don't come here again. I'm in here for my own peace of mind and you keep coming here and upsetting the balance."

She started to walk away.

"You said the killer was a woman," Smith shouted after her. "You got it wrong, Jessica. I thought you'd want to know. You got it wrong."

Jessica didn't turn round. She kept on walking. Smith watched as she carried on towards a small copse of trees.

"What was all that about?" Baldwin asked.

"She can't always be right," Smith replied. "She needed to know that she was wrong."

"Why?"

"I don't know why. She just needed to know, that's all."

His phone started to ring in his pocket. He took it out. It was Bridge.

"Sarge, we've got an ID on the dead guy. The photo in the paper reaped results. Five people have phoned in and mentioned the same name. Lenny Hall – thirty three years old."

"Do you have an address?"

"He lived in a council place on the Greentree Estate. Apparently he lived there with his sister, Beatrice."

Beatrice Hall, Smith thought.

The name seemed familiar.

"Beatrice Hall was one of the women on the list that Kelly Bowen gave us – the list of the women who were at the rehab centre at the same time. She's dead."

"According to two of the people who phoned in she's very much alive, Sarge."

CHAPTER FORTY SEVEN

What the hell is going on here? Smith drove as fast as he could to the address Bridge had given him for Lenny Hall and his sister Beatrice. *Beatrice Hall. She was on the list from the Weldon Centre. She was supposed to have died from cancer. Her brother is found dead in the river with a knife wound in the back of his neck. All the evidence found at the four murder scenes points in his direction.*
What the hell is going on?
Smith had instructed Bridge to speak with the director of the rehabilitation centre again. Yang Chu was to meet them at the Hall's residence. DI Brownhill wasn't answering her phone.
"Slow down," Baldwin warned. "You're going to have an accident."
Smith looked at the speedometer – he was approaching 100 miles per hour. He eased off on the accelerator. "The sister of the bloke who killed all those women – the one they pulled out of the river this morning, spent some time in the Weldon rehab place. She was there at the same time as four of the dead women and she's supposed to have died from cancer last year. Two people have phoned in claiming she's still alive. She could be at the address we're heading for now."
"What does all this mean?"
"It beats the hell out of me."

Smith drove into the Greenwood Estate. It was one of the few council estates left in the city that still housed council tenants – most of the old estates had been bought privately and renovated. Most of the houses in this estate looked exactly the same – bland grey buildings with roofs in need of repair. Many of the houses looked abandoned with their broken windows and overgrown gardens.

"This is the place here," Smith stopped outside one of the neater looking houses.

"You'd better lock your car door," Baldwin advised.

They got out and walked up the short path to the front door. Smith spotted Yang Chu's Ford Focus coming down the road. Yang Chu parked behind Smith's car and joined them on the doorstep.

Smith knocked on the door and waited.

Nothing.

He knocked again. He opened up the letterbox. "Beatrice, police. Please open the door."

"It looks like there's nobody home, Sarge," Yang Chu said.

"They haven't been home for days," a voice was heard from the road.

Smith turned to see a small child on an old bicycle. He was about ten years old.

"Who are you?" Smith asked.

"Bobby," the boy replied. "We live next door. Who are you? Debt collectors?"

"No. When did you last see Lenny and Beatrice?"

"Sunday, I think. Are you going to break their kneecaps? I heard Mr Dowthwaite at number 17 had his kneecaps done. He walks all funny now. Can I watch?"

"We're not going to break anybody's kneecaps. Do you know where your neighbours went?"

"No idea."

"Where are your mother and father?"

"Pub. Duh. It's Saturday."

With that he rode off down the road.

"What now, Sarge?" Yang Chu asked.

"Let's have a look inside," Smith said.

He tried the door. It wasn't locked.

"Sarge," Baldwin said. "Shouldn't we call it in?"

"There's nobody here, Baldwin, I just want to have a look around."

He opened the door wider and went in. A pile of what looked like bills and final reminders lay on the carpet underneath the door. Smith picked one up. It was addressed to Leonard Hall. On further inspection, Smith discovered that all of the correspondence was addressed to him. The house had a strange musty smell as though the place hadn't enjoyed fresh air for quite some time. Smith went through to the small kitchen at the end of the hallway. There was a pile of dirty dishes on the draining board by the sink.

"I'm going to take a look upstairs," he said.

He walked up the stairs. There were two bedrooms and a tiny bathroom. The bathroom was empty. There was no soap next to the bath nor toothbrushes in the glass on the edge of the sink.

They haven't been here for a while, Smith thought.

He checked the bedrooms. The first one was obviously used by Beatrice Hall – the faint smell of perfume still lingered in the air. The wardrobe was empty. The second bedroom contained just a single bed and a small cupboard. Smith opened the cupboard. Inside were a raincoat and a pair of slippers – very large slippers.

Size 13, Smith thought.

"It looks like they did a runner," Smith said to Baldwin and Yang Chu downstairs. "I want to speak to all of the neighbours. See if anybody knows anything."

An hour later, they'd spoken to everyone in the street who wasn't down the pub or at the Bookies and they'd drawn a blank. Nobody knew where the Halls had disappeared to. One elderly woman agreed with the story of the young boy with the kneecapping obsession – that they left some time the previous weekend, probably on the Sunday but she couldn't be one hundred percent sure.

"There's nothing more we can do here," Smith told Baldwin and Yang Chu. "I suggest we meet back at the station to go over all the new pieces of information. Maybe Webber has found something for us, too."

* * *

Spirits were higher than they'd been all week when Smith and the other detectives sat round the table in the conference room. Everybody felt as though they were finally starting to get somewhere – the pieces of the puzzle were being slowly put into place.

"Right," Brownhill said. "It's been a hell of a day. Sorry about the barbecue, Smith but you know how it goes. Leonard Hall killed at least two of those women. We'll know if he was responsible for the other two murders very soon."

"It was him," Bridge offered. "Unworthy. That pretty much settles it."

"We'll wait for forensics, nevertheless. Grant should have something for us within the hour. If it is confirmed that Leonard Hall was responsible for all four murders we'll have something we rarely get – a cut and dried case. Our murderer is now dead."

"Boss," Smith said. "Aren't you forgetting something?"

"Smith?"

"Our murderer was murdered. He had a four inch knife wound in the back of his neck. Somebody killed him."

"Whoever it was did us a favour," Yang Chu said.

"He was still the victim of a crime," Smith pointed out. "And we need to find out what happened to him."

"All in good time," Brownhill said.

Grant Webber entered the room. He was very red in the face.

"I thought I'd share the news in person," he panted. "Julie Phelps, Magda Collins, Joy Williams and Ashley White were all killed by the same person.

We compared previously unknown samples of hair to our Lenny Hall and we got a match. He was at all the crime scenes. We've got our Unworthy killer."

"It still doesn't tell us who killed Mr Hall," Smith wasn't going to let it lie.

"No it doesn't," Webber agreed. "But at least we've cleared one matter up."

"OK," Brownhill said. "With regards to the other matter, what did you find at the Hall's place?"

She addressed the question to Smith.

"The place has been abandoned," Smith said. "There's a stack of mail on the door mat and the place is empty. We spoke to the neighbours and nobody's seen Beatrice or Lenny Hall since last Sunday. They did a runner."

"Then we need to find this Beatrice Hall."

"There's something else," Smith said. "Beatrice Hall was on the list of women who were at the Weldon rehab centre at the same time." He looked over at Bridge. "What did the centre's director have to say about it?"

"Kelly Bowen," Bridge said. "She thought Beatrice was dead. She heard that she'd succumbed to cancer last year."

"She heard?"

"She said she had a phone call from someone telling her they thought she'd want to know that Beatrice had died."

"And who was this mystery caller?"

"Mrs Bowen couldn't recall a name."

"Great," Smith rubbed his temples. He sensed that a headache was on the way. "We need to find this Beatrice Hall. Somebody must know where she is."

"It's getting late," Brownhill said. "And it's been one hell of a day. I suggest we meet back here tomorrow morning and see what we can come up with. I must admit – this is all very strange. Four women are killed and our murderer conveniently turns up dead under our noses. This one has baffled the heck out of me. I'm exhausted."

"Me too," Baldwin said.

"I'll see you all back here tomorrow morning at eight."

CHAPTER FORTY EIGHT

Gregg Quinn rang the doorbell at 16 London Road for the third time. He took out his phone and dialled a number. The call went straight to voicemail. "Vanessa," he said. "I'm outside the house. Where are you? I've got a game of golf booked in half an hour and I can't take Sean with me. Let me know when you get this."

He put his phone back in his pocket and rang the bell again.

"Where's your mother hiding?" he asked his four year old son, Sean. "It's not like her not to answer the door."

The young boy put his hand on the door handle and turned it. The door was open.

"Why didn't I think of that?" Gregg said.

He went in first. "Vanessa. It's me. I've brought Sean back."

The house was silent.

He walked through to the kitchen. The sink was full of dirty dishes.

Something's wrong, Gregg thought, *Vanessa never leaves dirty dishes in the sink.*

The scream coming from the living room was something Gregg Quinn would never forget. He ran as quickly as he could to see why his four year old boy had reacted like he did.

Vanessa Quinn was lying on the carpet in front of the television. She was lying face down. Sean was holding her bloodstained hand. From the amount of blood on the carpet around her head, Gregg knew straight away that she was dead. He picked up his son and left the room. He hadn't noticed that the word *Unworthy* had been written on the wide-screen television set in blood.

Smith took the call ten minutes later. He was just about to leave home to go to the station.

"Smith," it was Brownhill. "Change of plan. Another woman has been killed. Vanessa Quinn. Her husband phoned the switchboard five minutes ago."

"Vanessa Quinn," the name was vaguely familiar.

Smith thought hard for a second. "She was on that list. She was in rehab the same time as the other women."

"Grant and his team are on their way." She gave Smith the address.

Smith's head was spinning as he drove to London Road. The man responsible for killing four women was dead and now another woman on the list of people who spent time at Weldon was also dead. He turned left and crossed the river. Pleasure cruisers were out in full force – tourists were enjoying what was left of the summer. He parked outside number 16 and got out. Webber's car was already there as was Yang Chu's Ford Focus. Yang Chu was talking to a middle aged man outside. A small boy was clinging to his trouser leg.

"Yang Chu," Smith said. "What have we got?"

"This is Gregg Quinn," Yang Chu nodded towards the man. "Vanessa Quinn's husband."

"We're separated," Gregg said. "I was bringing Sean back and that's when we found her. Sean found her. I'll never forget that scream. I don't know if he'll ever get over it."

"Mr Quinn," Smith said. "When was the last time you saw Vanessa?"

"I picked Sean up on Friday evening. I have him every second weekend. Who the hell would want to do that to Vanessa? She's never hurt anybody."

"We'll find out," Smith said and went inside the house.

Grant Webber was examining the huge television screen in the living room when Smith walked in. Vanessa Quinn was lying face down on the carpet.

"Morning, Webber," Smith said. "We must stop meeting like this."

"Come and look at this," Webber said.

Smith looked at the word written on the TV. "Unworthy. Looks like he killed her before someone killed him."

He moved closer to the woman on the carpet.

"Don't touch her," Webber warned. "I haven't had a chance to check her over yet."

"There's the murder weapon," Smith pointed to a shard of metal on the floor. "There's more broken pieces over there. Looks like what's left of a laptop. That piece has blood on it."

"You're sharp this morning," Webber scoffed. "What do you make of all this?"

"Unworthy. The woman spent time in rehab at the same time as the other dead women. She had a young child. Same pattern as the others. Like I say, it looks like the big bloke killed her and then somebody killed him."

"Would you mind leaving me and my crime scene in peace for a while?"

"Let me know what you find," Smith said. "Quick as you like."

He went back outside. An ambulance was parked behind his Ford Sierra. Yang Chu was still talking to Gregg Quinn.

"Sarge," Yang Chu said when Smith approached. "Can I have a word?"

They walked further up the road.

"What is it?" Smith asked.

"I spoke to Gregg Quinn," Yang Chu said. "And he told me something interesting."

"Go on."

"Vanessa Quinn spent time in the Weldon rehabilitation centre a while back."

"She was there at the same time as four of the other dead women. We already know that."

"Just wait. The women kept in touch afterwards. Gregg told me they got quite close during their time at the centre. They gradually stopped meeting but they stayed friends on Facebook. He said they'd share photos and experiences on a Facebook group. He reckons it was quite pathetic – they called themselves the Weldon Survivors."

"Weldon Survivors?" Smith repeated.

"That's right. I'll have to check the page of course but I think all of the dead women were on this Facebook group."

"Get onto it. I'm going to check in at the station. Webber has his hands full here – he's going to be a few hours. I'll need you to get a statement from Mr Quinn over there."

CHAPTER FORTY NINE

Smith found DI Brownhill in her office. She was busy on a phone call. Smith sat down opposite her and waited for her to end the call.
"Thank you," the DI said into the handset. "How long before you can confirm it one hundred percent?"
Her eyes lit up. "Let me know as soon as you have anything."
She ended the call. "That's interesting. Leonard Hall died sometime between eight and eleven on Thursday night."
"That can't be right," Smith said. "Vanessa Quinn's husband picked up their son on Friday evening. Vanessa was still very much alive."
"Then Leonard Hall didn't kill her."
"But the word Unworthy was written on the TV. This doesn't make sense."
"No it doesn't. Nobody knows about this calling card. The Unworthy part has been kept out of the press."
"This just get's odder and odder. We have a man who kills four women and leaves the word Unworthy at the murder scenes. Then someone kills him and two days later another woman is killed with the same word left at the scene. I don't know what to make of this."
"You and me both. The latest murder..."
"Vanessa Quinn, boss. Thirty two years old. She had a four year old boy. She spent time at the Weldon centre the same time as the other four dead women. Yang Chu found something worth checking out – they made a Facebook group where they shared all their news. The Weldon Survivors they called it."
"Weldon Survivors? I suppose it makes sense – they all went through rehab and came out of it better women for it."
"Yang Chu's checking it out. It still doesn't explain how Vanessa Quinn died or who killed her. If it wasn't the dead giant – who was it?"

"And who killed Leonard Hall?"

"And why?" Smith pondered. "Where's Bridge? I thought everyone was supposed to be in early this morning."

"Him and Baldwin have gone to speak to the director of the rehab centre again."

"Good idea."

"Any news on Leonard's sister, Beatrice?"

"Nothing. Someone told the director of the Weldon centre that she was dead. Why would somebody do that? What would they have to gain by pretending she was dead? Unless..."

"Unless what?"

Smith stood up. "I have to go and speak to somebody."

"Who?"

"Somebody who deserves an apology."

* * *

Smith made it to the Lemonwood hospital in less than five minutes. He wasn't sure what kind of reception lay in store for him – he'd been quite rude to Jessica Blakemore the last time he'd seen her. He approached the front desk. Joe, the old receptionist was back.

"Morning, Joe," Smith said. "What brings you back here?"

"Couldn't stay away," Joe replied. "They asked me to do a few weekend shifts – I miss the place and my social life sucks so I agreed. Are you here to see Jessica?"

"That's right."

"She's changed a lot since I was last here. I don't even know why she sticks around – there's nothing wrong with her."

"She has her reasons. Can I go through?"

"You know the way."

Smith stopped outside Jessica's door and waited. He wasn't exactly sure what he was going to say to her. Plus, the way he'd spoken to her the last time he was there was rather uncalled for. He knocked on the door. Jessica opened it and, seeing Smith there, slammed it shut again.

"Jessica," Smith said to the door. "I'm sorry. I was an arsehole last time. I really need your help."

He was relieved when the door opened again and Jessica nodded as an indication he was to come in.

"What do you want?"

"I'm sorry, Jessica," Smith said. "I didn't mean what I said last time – you're not losing your touch. You might just be able to help me crack this one."

"What are you going on about? Are you trying to get yourself committed in here?"

"Can you remember the first time we spoke about this Unworthy thing? One of the first things you mentioned was the word Unworthy was more something a woman would write. Can you remember that?"

"I'm insane – I'm not an idiot. Of course I remember. What of it?"

"The man who killed all those women is dead. Another woman was killed and Unworthy was written in blood on her TV. The man was already dead when she was killed."

"And nobody else knows about the Unworthy bit?"

"Nobody. That part was never released to the press."

"Tell me more."

"The dead man had a sister. She spent time at the same rehab centre as the five dead women. Last year someone phoned the centre and told the director she was dead. We searched the house where the sister and the dead man lived and it's empty. Nobody has seen them for a week."

"And the first woman was killed almost a week ago."

"That's right," Smith's brain was working overtime. "I think this is important. After what you said about the Unworthy part, I think we're getting close here."

"This dead man lived with his sister?"

"That's right."

"They were in it together."

Smith's phone started to ring. He answered it.

"Sarge," it was Yang Chu. "Can you talk?"

"Go on."

"I've had a look at that Facebook group. All of the dead women are on there. Julie Phelps, Magda Collins, Joy Williams, Ashley White and even the latest one – Vanessa Quinn. There's photos of their kids and all sorts. Details of their whole lives. It's an open group – there's no privacy settings. Anyone who owns a computer can access it."

Smith thought hard about the list of women who spent time at the rehab centre. "Who else is on the group?"

"A woman called Gloria Palmer and Erica Whitton. Not your Whitton of course – the one who lives in Harrogate."

"What does this other Erica Whitton look like?"

"That's the odd thing. There's photos of all the other women but none of this Erica Whitton."

"So this Facebook group has all the information about all these women?"

"Pretty much."

"This other woman – Gloria..."

"Palmer. Gloria Palmer."

"Does she have children?"

"Not as far as I can see, Sarge."

Smith ended the call and left the room without giving Jessica Blakemore any explanation.

His phone started to ring again as he walked down the corridor past the front next.

"See you soon," he said to Joe and answered his phone. "Smith."

"Sarge," it was Baldwin.

"What have you got?"

"We spoke with Kelly Bowen again and she told us something interesting. Beatrice Hall was only at the centre for a few days. And from what Mrs Bowen tells us, she was pretty much out of it most of the time."

"Out of it?"

"She didn't know who or where she was according to the director. She was in severe alcohol withdrawal. She checked herself out – she couldn't hack it."

The Weldon Survivors, Smith thought.

"Thanks, Baldwin," he said. "I need you to meet me at my house straight away."

"Sarge?"

"Just get there. Get hold of Bridge and Yang Chu and tell them to get there, too."

CHAPTER FIFTY

Whitton had just managed to get Laura to sleep for her morning nap when the doorbell rang. She sighed. She was looking forward to a relaxing cup of coffee and the Sunday papers. The two dogs were playing outside in the back garden. She walked down the hallway and opened the door.
"Good Morning," a blond woman in her thirties stood there. "Sorry to bother you but my phone's just died on me and I need to phone my brother to come and pick me up. Could I be a pain and use yours?"
"Of course," Whitton said. "I'll just go and get it."
She walked through to the kitchen. She didn't notice that the woman had come inside and closed the door behind her.
"What's the number?" Whitton picked up her phone from the kitchen table.
"It'll be easier if I dial it," the woman took the syringe from her pocket and stabbed it into Whitton's arm.
Whitton didn't have time to react. Within seconds her whole body became numb and she collapsed on the floor.

* * *

Smith looked at his speedometer – he was driving at almost one hundred miles an hour in a thirty zone. His heart was racing – he had a terrible feeling in his gut. He'd had the feeling before. His gut told him that Whitton was in serious danger. He sped past the Hog's Head and turned right onto the ring road. His house was still a few minutes away.
Beatrice Hall, he thought, *The Weldon Survivors.*

* * *

The woman bent over Whitton and felt for a pulse. It was strong.
"Good," she said. "I want you to know why – I want you to be awake when you die."

She laughed at her own paradoxical statement. She knew the drug would wear off in a few minutes and Whitton would soon wake up. She heard the sound of a car door slamming outside.

Smith ran up the path to his house, opened the door and went inside.
"Whitton," he shouted.
Nothing.
He could hear the two dogs barking outside in the back garden. He knew straight away there was something wrong.
He found Whitton on the kitchen floor.
"Whitton," he bent over her lifeless body and put his hand on her neck. She was still alive. He picked her up, carried her through to the living room and placed her on the sofa. He took out his phone and as he did so he felt a sharp pain in his back. It felt like somebody had stuck a red-hot poker through it. He felt another, more intense burning sensation and fell to the floor.

Yang Chu, Bridge and Baldwin all arrived at Smith's house at the same time. Seeing the front door wide open they went straight inside.
"Sarge," Yang Chu shouted. "Whitton!"
Bridge checked the kitchen while Baldwin and Yang Chu went in the living room.
"They're in here," Baldwin shouted.

The woman seemed to come out of nowhere. She punched Baldwin in the face with such a force that Baldwin lost consciousness for a few seconds. She lashed out at Yang Chu with the knife she'd used to stab Smith in the back with but the nimble DC was too quick. Yang Chu moved to the side.
"What the hell," Bridge came in the room.
He watched as Yang Chu kicked the woman in the kneecap. She screamed and fell to the floor.
"Help me get hold of her," Yang Chu yelled at Bridge.

He stood on the hand that was holding the knife and it was released from her grip. He kicked it to the other side of the room. Baldwin was still smarting from the blow to the head but she managed to help Bridge and Yang Chu yank the woman's hands behind her back and secure them with a set of handcuffs.

Whitton was starting to wake up. She didn't seem to grasp what was going on as she surveyed the scene in front of her. Smith was lying on his back on the carpet. From the amount of blood on the front of his shirt, it was clear that the injuries he'd sustained were serious.

"What happened?" Whitton managed to say.

"Smith told us to get here," Yang Chu told her. "He had a bad feeling. Looks like he got here just in time."

"He doesn't look too good," Bridge said. "I'm phoning for an ambulance." He looked at the handcuffed woman. "Get her out of here," he said to Yang Chu."Before I kill her myself."

CHAPTER FIFTY ONE
(*Two weeks later*)

The church was full to the brim. Bridge had arrived late and had to make do with a seat at the back next to Yang Chu. He spotted DI Brownhill near the front. She was sitting in between DCI Chalmers and Superintendant Smyth. Brownhill was crying – she wasn't even trying to hide it.
Bridge nodded to Yang Chu and whispered. "It's quite a turnout. I hope there'll be this many people at my funeral."
Yang Chu started to giggle. A man Bridge didn't recognise in the seat next to him cast him an admonitory glance.
"You're terrible," Yang Chu said.
"You're terrible, Sarge, if you don't mind."
"That's going to take a bit of getting used to."
Everybody, including Bridge himself had been surprised when he was given the detective sergeant post. Yang Chu had accepted defeat graciously.

The music started and everybody turned to look to the back of the church. Whitton walked in, escorted by her father. Smith stood at the altar. He was dressed in a suit and his arm was in a sling. He looked very pale. He'd been extremely lucky – the knife had narrowly missed his heart. A millimetre or two to the left and it would have been all over. He'd made a quick recovery considering the severity of the wounds.

Beatrice Hall had told them everything. The accident that left her unable to bear children had affected her more than she'd realised. She'd become obsessed with hatred for women who could have what she'd never be able to have. After her time in rehab, she'd come to resent even further the way women who, in her opinion weren't worthy of raising a child, were able to delight in motherhood. She blamed her brother and he accepted that blame – he humoured her every wish. He did what she told him to do. His only blunder was allowing Joy Williams' babysitter to see his face. He had to be disposed of. Whitton was supposed to be the last one. Hers was a simple case of mistaken identity – she bore the same name as one of the women who attended the Weldon Centre at the same time as her, it was as simple as that.

Whitton reached the front of the church and stood next to Smith.

"Wow," Smith said. "You scrub up alright for a copper."

Whitton smiled. "You don't look too bad yourself. Are you ready to do this?"

"Nope. But let's do it anyway."

THE END

ALSO BY STEWART GILES:

THE DS JASON SMITH SERIES –

- Smith
- Boomerang
- Ladybird
- Occam's Razor
- Harlequin
- Selene
- Horsemen
- Phobia

THE DC HARRIET TAYLOR SERIES -

- The Beekeeper
- The Perfect Murder

COMING SOON :

- The Backpacker

I hope you enjoyed reading. Please feel free to leave a review on Amazon or you can drop me a mail on starmarine@polka.co.za I will always reply to my emails, good or bad. Stewart.

Printed in Great Britain
by Amazon